To Emily,

♥

michelle
Weber
Hintz

To Emily,

♡

Mitchell
Weber

Calli Be
GOLD

Calli Be GOLD

Michele Weber Hurwitz

WENDY
LAMB
BOOKS

This is a work of fiction. Names, characters, places, and incidents either are the product of the author's imagination or are used fictiously. Any resemblance to actual persons, living or dead, events, or locales is entirely coincidental.

Text copyright © 2011 by Michele Weber Hurwitz
Jacket art copyright © 2011 by Linzie Hunter

All rights reserved. Published in the United States by Wendy Lamb Books, an imprint of Random House Children's Books, a division of Random House, Inc., New York.

Wendy Lamb Books and the colophon are trademarks of Random House, Inc.

Visit us on the Web! www.randomhouse.com/kids

Educators and librarians, for a variety of teaching tools, visit us at www.randomhouse.com/teachers

Library of Congress Cataloging-in-Publication Data
Hurwitz, Michele Weber.
  Calli be gold / Michele Weber Hurwitz — 1st ed.
    p. cm.
  Summary: Eleven-year-old Calli, the third child in a family of busy high-achievers, likes to take her time and observe rather than rush around, and when she meets an awkward, insecure second-grader named Noah and is paired with him in the Peer Helper Program, she finds satisfaction and strength in working with him.
  ISBN 978-0-385-73970-2 (hc : alk. paper) — ISBN 978-0-385-90802-3 (glb : alk paper) — ISBN 978-0-375-89823-5 (ebook) [1. Individuality—Fiction. 2. Self-confidence—Fiction. 3. Ability—Fiction. 4. Family life—Fiction. 5. Schools—Fiction.] I. Title.
  PZ7.H95744 Cal 2011
  [Fic]—dc22
                    2010013157

The text of this book is set in 12.5-point Adobe Caslon.
Book design by Vikki Sheatsley

Printed in the United States of America
10 9 8 7 6 5 4 3 2 1
First Edition

Random House Children's Books supports the First Amendment and celebrates the right to read.

To Ben, Rachel, Sam, and Cassie,
and to Mom

C'mon, Calli, Chop-chop

The way I look at it, you can divide all the people in the world into two categories: the loud ones who shout about who they are and what they do, and the quiet ones who just are and do.

I suppose one kind balances out the other kind, like black letters on white paper, or frozen teeth from a Popsicle on a ninety-five-degree summer day.

Except for this: if you're a quiet person randomly and hopelessly born into a family of louds, then it isn't a balance at all. It's downright lopsided.

Unfortunately, that would be me. Calli Gold, number three kid in the Gold family. One quiet. Four louds. Lopsided. Not to mention exasperating.

* * *

I am sitting at the kitchen table, sucking the salt from a sourdough pretzel nugget while my mom arranges pink and blue Post-it notes on the Calendar. Most of the salt is gone and the pretzel has turned to mush when I hear two bangs, several bumps, and one loud crash. My sister, Becca, has tumbled down the stairs.

I'm not surprised, and neither is Mom, because Becca trips on the stairs all the time. It's never anything serious, because she somehow grabs hold of the banister at the last second. I can't see her or the stairs from the kitchen, but I hear her groan and moan.

"You all right, Becca?" Mom calls out, still intently examining the dizzying pattern of pink and blue Post-its. She tugs at the back edge of her sweater, straightening the places where it's gotten bunched up.

I can picture Becca, sprawled at the bottom of the carpeted staircase, the stuff from her skating bag in a messy pile around her on the wood floor. Skates and towels and tights, and her sweatshirt proclaiming to the world that ICE GIRLS ARE SIZZLIN' HOT. And in the middle of it, with her lips pulled into a snarl, is my thirteen-year-old sister, mad at everyone who dares to look her way.

If Becca would ever listen to me (and she won't, because I'm only eleven), there are three things I would tell her: (1) Zip up the skating bag. Then everything won't fall out. (2) Socks can be awful slippery on carpeted stairs. And (3) It's probably not smart to look out the window by our front door to see if the cute boy across the street is shooting baskets in his driveway *and* walk down the stairs at the same time.

"Becca?" Mom calls again.

"I'm fine," she snaps.

Mom taps a pen on the enormous monthly write-on, wipe-off calendar taped to our kitchen wall. Better known as the Calendar. "It's going to be tight today," she says, peeling off one blue Post-it note and then a pink one. Pink are Becca's Post-its, and my brother Alex's are blue. These tiny squares contain their activity schedules down to the minute. My mother, who calls herself the Gold CFO (Chief Family Organizer), says that without her planning, our life as we know it would fall apart.

Mom used to be a project manager for a big food company, but for the time being, she says we are her projects. She says that managing this family is more work than her job ever was.

Light yellow is the color of my Post-its. There are only two of them on the Calendar for this month. One is for a dentist appointment and the other is for a haircut.

My dad says he'd like to see lots more yellow Post-its filling up the Calendar, because the Golds are busy people, and after all, I am a Gold too. Trouble is, in the past two years, I tried gymnastics, ballet, soccer, baton twirling, violin, and even origami, but I was a big disappointment in everything. Or everything was a big disappointment to me. I can't remember which. So as of right now, I haven't

3

yet made my mark on the Calendar. But Dad says I will. He says I have to, because I am a Gold.

Mom clicks the cap onto the pen and adjusts her glasses. "It's going to be really tight today," she repeats. Not only does Becca fall a lot, Mom often says things are going to be really tight. When she says this, the up-and-down crease between her eyebrows becomes deeper.

"Get yourself together, Becca," Mom shouts. She scans the pink Post-it in her hand. "We have eight minutes to get you to skating." She turns to me. "Do you have homework, Calli?"

"I finished it."

She raises her eyebrows. "All of it?"

"Yep." I pop another pretzel into my mouth. "At school."

"Don't you have a math test coming up?"

"We reviewed in class."

"Well then," she says, "bring a book along. Or go over a few more problems for the test. I know you get a little bored at the rink, and I can't entertain you today. I have a meeting with the other skating moms. You know I'm chairing the costume committee this year. We have a lot of crucial information to go over. *Crucial*," she repeats, like I hadn't heard the first time.

She grabs her purse from the counter and pulls her keys from one of the pockets. Her purse isn't a regular purse; it's more like a miniature suitcase, with all kinds of compartments and pockets and zippers and pouches. Metallic silver, the thing weighs a ton. I know. I've tried to pick it up.

She isn't one of those mothers who can never find anything in their purses, like my friend Wanda's mom, who's always searching for Kleenex, money, or Chap Stick. Dad brags that Mom can locate something in her purse with the accuracy of a global satellite.

"Mom?" I say, crossing my legs importantly like she does. "Do I have to go to the rink? Can't I stay home? I think I'm old enough to stay by myself now." I take a deep breath. "Wanda's mom has started to let her stay by herself."

She puts a hand on her hip and gives me one of those unblinking mom stares, the kind that signals the asking of an outrageously dumb question.

"No," she says, "you cannot stay home by yourself. I don't care what Wanda does. You know that the rule in *this* family is eleven and a half, no more, no less. Don't start with me today, Calli, I don't have time for this." She snaps her purse closed and turns away. Discussion over.

I sigh, sink lower in my chair, and put another pretzel into my mouth as Becca limps dramatically into the kitchen. "I think I hurt my ankle," she whimpers. "I don't know if I can skate today." She drops her bag and one skate topples out, thudding across the tile floor.

Becca never enters a room calmly. She always drops

something, smashes into something else, falls, yells, whines, or creates what Grandma Gold calls a "ruckus." Becca always seems to have a lot of injuries too.

"Becca, you are absolutely fine." Mom rolls her eyes and glances over at me. I can't help it: a little giggle escapes.

Becca whips her head in my direction. "What's your problem? You think it's funny that I can barely walk?"

"No," I say quickly.

Dropping to the floor, Becca shoves the skate back inside her bag, then begins the process of gathering her dark hair into a high ponytail. She spent an hour last night straightening it with a flat iron, but still, she smooths it over and over in upward strokes, even though it already seems to be completely smooth. Her brown eyes are lined with thick black eyeliner, and her lids are smothered in bright glittery blue. I want to tell her she's pretty without that stuff, but just like with my staircase advice, I know she won't listen.

"Becca, can you do your hair in the car?" Mom asks, looking a bit annoyed. "We're late as it is, and you know those coaches. . . ." She taps her watch. "Let's go, before they kick you off the team."

Becca gives me a slight shove after she pulls herself up from the floor. "Alex and I didn't get to stay by ourselves when we were your age," she says. "Why should you get special privileges just because you're the baby of the family?" She crosses her arms in front of her chest and raises her eyebrows, as if daring me to come up with an answer.

I don't.

"Put the pretzels away," Mom tells me. Then she claps her hands and says those words I dread. "C'mon, Calli, chop-chop."

"Chop-chop" means we have to take my brother or sister somewhere, and I get to sit in the way back of a minivan that hasn't been washed in a very long time and watch my life whiz past through a grimy, sticky, steamed-up window.

"We haven't got all day," Mom adds.

I clip the pretzel bag, return it to the pantry, then grab my jacket and follow them into the garage. Becca is hobbling in front of me, dragging her skating bag across the dusty floor. "It might be nice if one of you could give me a hand here," she complains, but Mom plops onto the driver's seat and motions for me to climb in back.

Before I'm even buckled, Mom zooms backward out of the driveway. She drives too fast, because we're always late and rushing to get somewhere. Plus she has this habit of tacking the day's Post-it notes to the steering wheel, and she keeps glancing down at them instead of paying attention to her driving.

After Becca finally finishes her ponytail, she announces, "By the way, I'm out of lead."

"Lead?" Mom asks as the car veers to the right. "You mean the kind for a mechanical pencil?"

"Yes," Becca answers, "and I have *so* much homework tonight."

Mom glances in the rearview mirror. "I don't know if I'll have time to get your lead today. Can't you just use a regular pencil?"

Becca sneers. "I don't think so."

"Mom?" I jump in. "I need something for school too."

She sighs and makes a sharp turn. "Didn't we get you everything you needed for school back in August?"

"Mrs. Lamont said we needed a new spiral notebook. For something special."

"Well, if you're going to get her a spiral, you can get my lead," Becca interrupts.

"Enough, you two. I'll see how my timing is later."

The clock on the dashboard says 4:57. Mom speeds up. Becca's practice starts at five. I turn to the window and wipe in a circle with my fingers, clearing the glass. The late October sky is patched with skinny streaks of pink and purple and orange. It reminds me of rays and line segments in geometry, all those intersecting angles and shapes in sunset colors. I don't bother to point this out to Mom and Becca, who are arguing about Becca's supposedly twisted ankle. I know by now that I'm the only one in the Gold family who notices things like that.

Mom swerves into a parking space and I follow her and my sister through the doors of the skating rink.

I know by now that I'm the only one in the Gold family who notices a lot of things.

Noah on the Floor

The skating rink looks the same as it always does: dark and dull and gray. It has a mixed aroma of smelly feet and burnt popcorn from the concession stand. There isn't a single window in the entire place, and the floor is covered in black rubber so the skaters can walk around without damaging their blades.

Every time I'm here, I look up at the neon orange banner with the first initials and last names of the skaters from last year's team. It hangs brightly from the ceiling. Becca's is right in the center: B. GOLD. I can't help thinking the banner proclaims my family's philosophy—Be Gold . . . because why would you be anything else?

A plaque hangs in the gym where my brother, Alex, played travel basketball last year. It has the names of all the players on his team, plus a listing of their winning record, game by game. So that one says A. GOLD and even has a photo of the team above the names.

Dad is very proud of the B. Gold banner and the A. Gold plaque and he tells everyone about them. There is yet to be a C. Gold banner or plaque or even a small ribbon anywhere in town, but Dad says my time is coming and I will soon find my passion.

Becca flounces over to her teammates and throws her bag on the floor. They look like identical copies of each other, with their huffy expressions, black eyeliner, glittery eye shadow, and high, straight-haired ponytails. While Becca starts getting her skates on, Mom and the other skating mothers take over a few tables near the concession stand. They spread out their folders and papers, sip from cups of coffee, and talk on their cell phones. They look serious, because as Mom says, synchronized skating is very important business. I wonder if all these mothers were once project managers too.

A few of them are wearing their black satin jackets with SYNCHRONETTES MOM sewn in loopy letters on the back. That's the name of Becca's team: the Synchronettes. When the girls and the moms and the coaches all huddle together in their matching jackets before a competition, they look like a small army ready to take on the entire world.

The usual skating rink siblings are here: Jeremy and Jordan, the five-year-old twin boys who race to the fountain, then shoot water at each other through the spaces in their teeth; the black-haired kid who wears black jeans and a black hoodie that says DEATH RULES, and never talks to anyone; and the little blond toddler who always has food stains on her face and wails nonstop.

The coach of the skating team marches over and I hear her shout, "Let's go, girls. We have a lot to get through today!" Becca says this year's coach is brutal. Her name is Coach Ruth but the girls call her Coach Ruthless. Becca never looks very happy when she's coming here or when she's on the ice, so I'm not sure why she skates. Wouldn't it be better to find something she really likes to do? More of my advice she'll never listen to.

As the girls parade off after Coach Ruthless, I wander over by the area everyone calls the arcade. It's really just three old, beat-up video games. There are one of those unwinnable prize machines with the crane, a hockey-foosball game that barely works, and a car-racing game with an accelerator that's permanently stuck to the ground because Jeremy and Jordan jam wads of gum behind it every week.

I'm watching the screen of the racing game, which keeps showing a car that veers off the track, rams into a wall, and explodes, when I realize I forgot to bring a book. I'm going to have nothing to do for an hour and a half. A mixture of mad and sad comes over me, but then something unusual catches my eye. I see a kid lying completely still under the hockey-foosball game. He's small and skinny, maybe about seven or eight, wearing a dark blue winter jacket and jeans.

I know all of the skating team's little brothers but I've never seen this kid before. I walk over to the hockey-game table and circle it a few times to see if he stirs. Finally, I crouch down and take a close-up look. He's still lying perfectly motionless and I'm not even sure if he's breathing. Behind his gold-wire-framed glasses, his eyes are closed. His hair is kind of messy, like he never combed it this morning. Uneven spikes of light brown stick up in lots of directions. No one else seems to have noticed him. I feel a little worried. What if he fainted or got sick? Where is his mom, or dad, or babysitter? And why is he wearing a winter jacket? It's not even that cold out.

"Excuse me," I say softly. "Hey? Are you okay?"

No response.

"Are you sick or something? Did you hurt yourself?" I gently place my hand on top of his jacket.

No answer. Maybe he just fell asleep.

"Do you want me to get someone?" I ask. "Is your mom here?"

Nothing.

I decide to tell Mom about the kid. When I reach her, she's deep in conversation with one of the other skating team mothers. I wait politely at her side until I can't stand it anymore. "Mom," I say quietly. She looks at me sort of vacantly. "Mom, there's this kid . . ." I point in the direction of the arcade.

"Calli," she sighs. "I'm in the middle of a conversation. Can it wait?"

"But, Mom," I plead, "he's lying on the floor and . . . what if something's wrong?"

She has already turned back to the other mom and I'm sure she didn't hear me. "Barb," she says, "the costumes were supposed to be sapphire with rhinestones, not some drab blue with a few splatters of glitter! This is a huge mistake and we don't have time to reorder. The first competition is in less than eight weeks!"

I wait another few seconds but Mom keeps talking. I walk back to the hockey game, and sure enough, the kid's still there. I don't know what to do, so I wander inside the rink and watch Becca's team for a few minutes. They're practicing their pass-through, a pretty cool move where two parallel lines of skaters head toward each other like they're going to crash; then the lines weave through each other. Becca looks grumpy, and I can see big wet spots on the knees of her tights, which means she fell. Coach Ruthless looks aggravated and mad.

In the last two years, Becca's team never scored high enough in any competition to beat the Lady Reds, the regional champs, but Ruthless says this season is going to be different. I heard Becca tell Dad that the coach was "out for blood," which sounded kind of scary to me. Dad's response was "Well, you want to win, don't you?"

The team finishes the routine and Ruthless stops the music. "Again," she demands, and the girls skate back to their starting positions. "Gold," I hear Ruthless call out. "Over here." She points to a spot on the ice next to where she's standing. Becca skates over and stops, then rubs the backs of her arms like she's cold. I can't hear anything, but the coach is talking to Becca, and Becca's not saying a word. The coach has her back to me, so I can't see her face, but if I took a guess, I'd bet she isn't complimenting Becca on her eye makeup.

I go back to the arcade, and the kid still hasn't moved an inch. I bend down again and gently shake his shoulder. "Listen, please tell me if you're okay," I say. "'Cause I'm getting a little concerned here."

After a few seconds, this tiny voice, muffled and quiet-sounding, says, "Go away."

I'm so startled that I jerk upward and bang my head on the edge of the game table. As I'm rubbing the spot that is sure to grow into a goose egg, the kid squirms and wriggles and drags a sleeve across his nose, then goes back to lying completely still.

When he moved, his jacket opened a little, and I can read the tag that says THIS JACKET BELONGS TO. The name written below, in black marker, is Noah Zullo.

"Is that your name?" I ask, still rubbing my head. "Noah Zullo?"

He doesn't respond.

"Do you have a sister on the skating team?" I ask.

Noah Zullo ignores me.

"Fine. Okay. Lay here for the rest of your life if that's what you want to do."

I stomp away and think about Wanda and Claire, my best friends since kindergarten, and how they're probably all cozy and warm inside their calm, quiet houses, eating delicious home-cooked dinners. Probably with a pie or peppermint ice cream for dessert. Wanda has one brother and he's away at college. Claire is an only child and her dad is always going on business trips, to somewhere like India or Ireland or Indonesia. I can't remember—something with an "I."

Claire's dad brings her a present every time he comes home. She has collections of snow globes, dolls from other countries, and miniature glass animals. They sit on her bookshelves and no one can shake them or play with them or touch them, not even Wanda or me. My guess is Claire doesn't touch them either. She just stares at them with a sad face, especially during the long weeks when her dad is gone. I've never asked her about it, but I have a feeling she'd rather have her dad around instead of the collections.

I sink into a chair at one of the empty tables in the concession area and find a newspaper that someone left behind. I flip to the comics and read my favorites, only three strips, but none of them are very funny today.

Mom and the other black-satin-jacket mothers are still busy with their work, chattering and jotting notes and handing each other papers. Jeremy and Jordan have flooded the floor underneath the fountain, and one of the guys from the rink is mopping up the water. The black-haired, black-jeaned hoodie kid is now skulking around with a pair of black sunglasses on, circling the rink like a lion in a zoo.

All of a sudden, I notice a dad I've never seen before, in the last booth by the wall. He's typing on a laptop and seems to be talking to himself. Then I realize he has one of those phone-earpiece things clipped around his ear. He's wearing a white shirt and a striped red tie and keeps repeating, "Not a problem," and then, "Will do."

I wonder if he could be Noah Zullo's dad. I lean out from the table to check if Noah's still under the hockey game, and sure enough, he's there. If this is his dad, I'm certain he doesn't know where Noah is. Does anyone besides me know where Noah is?

The way he looks, forlorn and alone under that table, reminds me for some reason of an old woman I saw once who was trying to get a cart in the grocery store. The woman had a cane and she was trying to pull out the one in the front from the big row of carts but it was stuck. Everyone was running into and out of the store and no one noticed her. I wanted to stop and help her get a cart, but Mom grabbed my arm and said, "Chop-chop!" By the time we left the store, she was gone. I know it was just a little thing and it's silly to think about, but I always wondered if the woman ever got her cart, or if she just gave up and went home.

Exactly when the girls on Becca's team start parading from the doors of the rink, the skating moms collect their papers and folders, stand up, and throw away their empty cups. The girls sprawl on the floor and begin to pull off their skates and wipe the shiny blades with towels. A few of them are whispering to each other.

Mom looks over in my direction. "Get your jacket on, Calli. We've got to run."

I sigh.

Of course we do.

What else would we do?

Take It to the Hoop!

Back in the van, as we head toward the high school to watch my brother's basketball game, Becca insists that she has to be dropped off at home because her ankle is throbbing. "I need an ice pack," she whines. "Plus," she says, glancing back at me, "*I* am in seventh grade, and unlike someone in this car who is in fifth grade, *I* have tons of homework. My teachers are insane. Two tests tomorrow, a quiz the day after, a project due next week, and a paper to write by Friday."

She huffs importantly, but I don't say anything, and neither does Mom, who is driving like a maniac, so Becca says snippily, "Is anybody listening to me? Does anybody care?" She loosens her ponytail and lets her hair fall around her shoulders, then fluffs it out with her fingers.

Mom careens into the driveway and pushes the button

to open the side door of the van for my sister. "Of course I'm listening," Mom tells Becca as she tumbles out, pulling her skating bag along with her. "Go ahead and get started on your homework. I want to get to Alex's game before the third quarter starts. But do me a favor. Turn the oven to the 'warm' setting at seven o'clock. I've got a lasagna cooking. We should be home around seven-thirty."

Before Becca is even inside the house, Mom is racing back out of the driveway, looking down at the blue Post-it attached to the steering wheel.

Ten minutes is about all it takes to drive to the high school, because everything is pretty close in Southbrook. I've lived here my entire life and I've always wondered why our village was named Southbrook. There are some man-made ponds around here, but I've never seen a single brook, except if you count the trickle of water that runs behind the baseball field when it rains a lot.

Maybe Southbrook was a name that sounded appealing. Would people have wanted to live here if the town was called Southtrickle? Probably not.

The high school parking lot is crowded and we have to park far away from the entrance to the gym. Mom says those words again as I'm stepping out of the van: "C'mon, Calli, chop-chop." Then she zips her jacket and grabs my hand. Together we jog to the gym door and open it to the sounds of the basketball game.

Mom pants a little. Not because she's out of shape,

but because she's often doing so many things at the same time. She doesn't just multitask; she multi-lives. Our life, she says, is one big rush. Then she always adds cheerfully, "One big Gold rush!" She tells us she wouldn't have it any other way.

We see Dad in his suit and tie, pacing back and forth near one end of the bleachers. Mom marches up to him, her purse swinging from her hand like an enormous lantern. "Larry! I got here as quickly as I could. What's going on?" she demands.

"Tied at the half," he answers. He looks all sweaty and red in the face, like he just finished running a marathon.

"Hi, Dad," I say softly. He glances down at me and rumples my hair, then turns back to Mom. The two of them discuss the game as if it's life-or-death.

"How's he playing?" Mom asks, her voice low.

"He's on fire," Dad tells her. "Unbelievable today!"

"How many points?"

"Fourteen."

She looks at the scoreboard. "We're in foul trouble?"

Dad throws his arms into the air. "Those refs," he snorts. "They're blind! Called him on four fouls. They've got it out for him, there's no doubt about that. He's the most aggressive player on the court, so they're watching his every move."

Mom nods while he continues ranting. "I'm filing a complaint about these refs," he says. "They're the worst I've ever seen."

I spot Alex on the bench, guzzling from a bottle of red Gatorade. My brother is a freshman, and he is on the A team, which is supposed to have the best players. If you ask me, though, the *A* stands for "attitude," which is something Alex seems to have a lot of these days. Two cheerleaders are looking at him, waving and giggling. They have the same flat, straight hair as Becca, tied in ponytails with green and gold ribbons, the school colors. Alex puts down the bottle and wipes a towel across his forehead. I wave to him, but I don't think he sees me.

One of our neighbors was a high school cheerleader when Alex and I were little. Alex used to pull me around the block in our wagon, and sometimes when we'd pass her house, she'd be out front in her cheerleader uniform, practicing her routines. I was only five, but I remember Alex telling me that cheerleaders were silly and dumb and I should have higher aspirations. I didn't know what "aspirations" meant, but he said I was too smart to do all the cheering for boys and should cheer for things I could do myself.

I remember thinking Alex was the best big brother in the world that day, but now I see that he's smiling back at the two cheerleaders, and this makes my heart hurt and feel as heavy as Mom's purse.

A loud horn blows, and I jump. "The second half is starting," Dad says nervously, rubbing at his forehead.

"You staying down here?" Mom asks.

"You know I can't sit during his games, Karen."

Dad resumes his pacing and sweating while Mom climbs up the bleachers and takes a seat. She motions for me to follow. Alex's team strolls onto the court and my brother throws a glance in our direction. Dad mouths something to him and Alex nods. Must be some sort of secret fatherly basketball advice.

As the game starts up, I sit down next to Mom. "Take your jacket off, Calli," she urges. "You're going to get overheated. It's warm in here."

"I'm fine," I mutter, and sit there unmoving in my jacket.

The gym is crowded and noisy and everyone seems to be yelling something at someone.

Still, I can clearly hear Dad's voice above the rest. "Drive!" he roars as my brother dribbles the ball down the court. "Take it to the hoop!" he shouts as Alex weaves around two players from the other team. Alex looks over at Dad although the coach is shouting something at him. "Shoot!" Dad screams.

Dad's face is so frantic and red he reminds me of a crazed cartoon character, like his eyes might pop out of their sockets or steam will shoot out of his ears.

It's fair to say that Dad becomes possessed when he's watching Alex play basketball. Same thing when he watches Becca skate in a competition. He forgets about the rest of the world. If a fire was to start in the bleachers, he wouldn't even notice.

Alex takes a long shot, then throws his fists into the

air as the ball sinks through the net. The crowd erupts. The cheerleaders do little cutesy jumps. Mom bolts up from her seat like a rocket and sends me off balance, toppling me backward from the bench. She doesn't realize she knocked me over, because she's applauding wildly and stamping her feet and yelling, "Woo, woo!"

Here I am, stuck with my legs up on the bench and the rest of me below. All around me, people's feet are tapping and stomping, shaking the bleachers like a mini earthquake.

With the deafening commotion, people crammed into their seats, Dad shooting imaginary steam from his ears, and Mom woo-wooing, all under the glaring overhead lights of the high school gym, for some reason, the only thing I can think about is that little kid at the rink, Noah Zullo, lying quiet and still and alone in his zipped-up jacket under the broken hockey-foosball table.

I wonder who he is and why he was at the rink. I wonder if he's still there, under the table, or if someone found him and took him home. Then I wonder why I'm wondering so much about him.

Burnt Lasagna

The other team ties up the game right at the ending buzzer. Ugh. Overtime. Everyone gets even crazier. Dad starts to climb toward us, then stops as a father from the other team shouts that Alex's team is a bunch of punks. Dad yells a couple of swears in his direction. Then the other father asks Dad if he wants to "take it outside," but a woman next to him, probably his wife, plunks a hand on his shoulder and pushes him down onto the bleacher seat. A different woman shouts to both fathers that they are setting a bad example and should shut up unless they want to get thrown out of the gym.

I'm noticing all the things no one else notices, like how the dad who called Alex's team punks has an unusual striped pattern of baldness and hair, and how the woman who told them to shut up has eyebrows that are colored in thickly with brown pencil.

I'm curious about whether the man combs his hair to get it like that, or if it naturally grows that way, and if the woman puts on the eyebrow pencil every morning and how it stays untouched all day.

At last, the game has only a few seconds left. After some more fouls and free throws and time-outs, when my stomach grumbles are sounding as loud as thunder, the game finally ends. Alex's team wins by two points. Do I need to say who made the final shot?

Finally, the four of us are walking through the dark parking lot to Mom's van and Dad's car. Dad is more leaping than walking, really, as he slaps Alex on the back and punches his fist upward in the night air. "Now that's how it's done!" he shouts ecstatically. "You dominated that entire game. Alex, my boy, that might have been the best of your career!"

Then, right in the middle of the parking lot, Dad stops and grabs Alex's shoulders. "I've never been more proud of you, Son," he says. He chokes up a little and his eyes look misty. I wonder if he's going to cry.

Mom's eyes are shining too as she beams at Alex and pulls a tissue from one of her purse compartments. "Remember this moment," she tells him, dabbing at her eyes. "They don't get any better than this."

"That shot, at the end . . ." Dad glows. "It was amazing.

I thought it might hit the rim but it was right on target." Dad starts talking about different shots and defensive moves that Alex made throughout the game. He always does this—relives every single second of Alex's games, or Becca's competitions—for days afterward sometimes, like everything else in life isn't worth a sentence.

Alex listens and nods and smiles; then Mom and Dad both lean toward him and give him about twenty-five hugs apiece. Finally, he shrugs them off and says, "I'm hungry. Let's go."

I look up at my brother. "Good job, Alex," I say, and he swats me softly on the back.

"Hey, Cal," he says. When he smiles at me, my heart feels a little lighter.

We start walking again and I see how many red and yellow leaves have fallen around the parking lot, trampled on in the rush of everyone leaving the game. The air feels cooler and I make a secret wish for an early first snow this year so Wanda, Claire, and I can go sledding on our favorite hill across from the junior high.

On the car ride home, Mom calls Grandma Gold to tell her about Alex's victory. I can hear Grandma's voice clearly from the speakerphone, because wouldn't you know it, she's pretty loud too.

"Well, of course! I wouldn't have expected anything less," Grandma Gold shouts. She then says that Alex's basketball talent definitely comes from the Gold side of the family. "My Joel could have played in college, you know."

Mom looks a little annoyed. "Larry played basketball too," she says.

"Not past freshman year in high school," Grandma Gold reminds us. "Joel had the goods. But what can you do? Medicine was calling."

I met Uncle Joel only a few times, when I was little, and I don't remember him. He lives in California. Dad says he's very busy being a plastic surgeon to the stars.

"E-mail me Alex's schedule," Grandma says. "I'll see if I can get to a game one of these days when I'm not tied up with mah-jongg."

"Okay," Mom replies. Then she ends the call and I hear her mutter, "Joel never really could have played in college. What is she saying?"

"Mom?" I ask as we pull into the garage. "Don't forget I need that spiral."

"I didn't forget," she says.

When she turns off the car, she sniffs suspiciously like she's some sort of police dog, then exclaims, "Something's burning!" She runs into the house, drops her purse onto the counter, and races to the oven.

"Becca!" she yells, jerking open the oven door. Smoke pours out and fills the air, and Mom starts waving her hands frantically through the thick haze. "Did I or did I not tell her to turn the oven to 'warm' at seven o'clock?" she groans, looking at me.

"You did," I answer quietly, coughing a little from the

burning cloud of smoke hanging in the air. The oven clock says 8:15.

Becca stumbles into the kitchen and says, "Oops," as Mom removes a glass pan holding a very burnt, very blackened, very crisp-looking lasagna.

"Would you look at this?" Mom fumes, setting the pan down and parking both hands on her hips. Her glasses fog up and her eyes sort of disappear for a minute. She pins her lips together tightly and marches over to a drawer. She pulls out a spatula and jabs at the top of the crusted lasagna.

"So what! Aren't I allowed to forget something once in a while?" Becca stamps a foot. "You don't understand! I'm under a lot of stress right now!"

She flounces from the kitchen, tripping on her way out, as Dad and Alex come in from the garage. The four of us stare at the lasagna.

"Well," Mom says sharply, "we'll just have to deal with it. This is dinner tonight, because I don't have time to cook anything else."

Within five minutes, we are all sprawled around the table. Alex is shoving crackers into his mouth, Dad is still beaming about the last shot of the game, Becca contorts her face and props her ankle on an empty chair, and Mom is sawing off uneven chunks of the hardened lasagna and plunking them onto plates.

Despite the fact that we are struggling to cut off a bite of lasagna, let alone chew it, Dad says we should make

the best of the situation and he begins the usual dinnertime ABC game. We are named in alphabetical order—
Alex, Becca, Calli—and every night, Dad goes from child
to child, asking us what we accomplished that day.

There have been times I've wanted to ask my parents
if they thought this through fully when they named their
children. Didn't they consider the consequences of having a third child who would forever be branded a *C*? I
know they thought it was cute and clever. But I bet if one
of them was number three with a *C,* they would see
things quite differently.

"A-man," Dad calls to my brother, who answers,
"Wha?" and dribbles cracker crumbs from his mouth,
which makes Becca cringe and moan, "Ew! Do you have
to be so disgusting?"

"Huge accomplishment today." Dad compliments
Alex for the hundredth time. "Winning a critical game.
Playing your best. I'll tell ya, Son, you're the whole team."

"Yeah." Alex grins, slurping from his glass of soda
pop. "Plus I got an A on my biology test." He wipes the
back of his hand across his mouth.

"Alex, your napkin is right in front of you." Mom
picks it up and waves it near his face.

"Way to go," Dad says, and high-fives Alex. He turns
to Becca and peers over at her ankle. "Injury? That's the
life of a skater. You need to be tough. To skate with the
big girls, you gotta take the pain."

She rolls her eyes.

"Daily accomplishment?" he says to her, as if we are all in one of his big company meetings.

"My skating team finally got the pass-through down," Becca announces, smiling for maybe the first time today. "Ruthless was actually happy with us."

I lick my lips and swallow. My turn is coming. My forehead feels hot and my palms grow sweaty.

"In fact," Becca adds, "she pulled me aside today to tell me how well I'm skating. She said if I continue like this, I'll move up to the higher team next year for sure."

"There you go," Dad says, banging his fist on the table. The dishes and glasses clatter. "See? Hard work, determination, never giving up. That's what it's all about. Don't I always say you can do whatever you set your mind to in this world?

"And," he continues, looking in my direction, "what kind of accomplishment can you report today, Miss Calli?"

Everyone looks at me.

What should I answer? I tried to help some kid lying under the hockey-game table but he didn't want my help. I finished all my homework at school, then I rode around with Mom in the van and watched Becca's practice and Alex's game and noticed the streaks of color in the sky.

"Well," I say.

"Yes?" Dad asks, gnawing on a piece of the lasagna.

"Um . . ."

He smiles and reaches over to rumple my hair like he did at the basketball game. Then he tucks his hand under my chin and lifts it a bit. "There's always tomorrow," he says kindly. "I know you'll have something big to report one day."

The thing is, I'm not so sure anymore.

On my fourth-grade report card, my teacher described me as "nice and pleasant, an average student." Dad hit the roof. "We are the Golds! We're golden!" he boomed at me. "No Gold is average!" His face was flushed and puffy, like I had done something really wrong, something against the law maybe. Not the real law, but the Gold law. That was when they started me on all the activities—the gymnastics and violin and all that. Even though nothing has worked so far, Dad says finding a passion can take time and he keeps reassuring me that I just haven't hit on the right thing yet. Soon, he says, I will have lots of Post-its and accomplishments too.

Alex stabs his chunk of lasagna with his knife and raises it above his head, making Dad and Becca laugh. "Ladies and gentlemen, here we have the first ever radio-active lasagna," Alex says, and even Mom laughs then. The rest of them pick up their lasagnas with their knives and they all crack up in unison, but I just sigh to myself.

Being a part of this family reminds me of the baby chicks I saw once at an exhibit at the science museum in the city. On one side of an incubator were eggs that hadn't hatched yet, but on the other side, there were lots of newly hatched baby chicks. They were funny and fluffy and I could have watched them for hours.

A girl was shaking a charm bracelet close to the window, and the chicks were going crazy, chirping and running around and bumping into each other. But there was one chick that was simply sitting in the middle of the commotion, huddled in its feathers, not moving, just blinking its tiny eyes. I wanted to reach inside and gather up that quiet little chick in my hand and tell it I understood completely.

Mom opens the tub of margarine and smears a glob across a piece of bread. I can tell she's ready to burst out with her list of accomplishments, because, as she often reminds us, even though she's not working outside the home, that doesn't mean she's not achieving things too.

She clears her throat proudly and we all look her way. "My turn," she says. "I found out the PTO raked in over one thousand dollars on the school clothing sale. The sale I coordinated, mind you. And, the costume company sent us the wrong costumes for Becca's skating competition, but we brought it to their attention and they're making the right ones for free. So the girls will actually have two costumes!"

Dad applauds for her and she stands up at the table and takes a bow.

"Way to go, Karen," Becca drones.

"Thank you," she says, "and by the way, 'Mom' would be just fine."

A few minutes later, the usual after-dinner rush begins. Mom starts clearing dishes. Alex's cell phone rings, and I gather from the lowering of his voice that one of the cheerleaders is on the other end. Becca begins to complain again about her ankle and asks me in an overly sweet voice to get her a cookie.

I bring her the package of Oreos and she takes the last two. "Mom," she moans, pulling one apart. "Do we have any crutches?"

Mom purses her lips. "No, we do not, and I doubt you need crutches. Your ankle looks fine. It's not even swollen. Rest up and you'll be good as new tomorrow."

"How do you know?" Becca huffs. She licks the white Oreo filling and dumps the cookie ends onto her plate. "When did you get your medical degree?"

Mom doesn't reply to that. Everyone knows better than to start up with Becca at a time like this.

"Help me with the dishes, Calli?" Mom says. "As long as you've got nothing else to do."

Alex and Dad drift away, and Becca finally hobbles out of the room. My sister is way past being a drama queen. She's more like a drama empress.

At last, the kitchen is calm, with just Mom and me. I carry a stack of dishes from the table and set them to the side of the sink. "Mom?" I ask. "Can I tell you about what we did in science today?"

She nods absentmindedly and starts filling the lasagna pan with water, sloshing it around with her hand.

"We talked about how all the ice is melting in the Arctic."

33

"Mmm-hmm," she says, reaching for the bottle of soap.

"It's scaring me," I admit. "What will happen to the polar bears and all the other animals?"

She pushes a strand of hair out of her face with the back of her hand. "I'm sure they'll find a way to survive."

"No, see, that's just it. They won't. They need the ice to live. That's what they said in this movie we watched."

She tips the pan over and dumps out the murky water.

"All those animals could become extinct," I tell her.

"That's probably an exaggeration. I doubt it will really happen."

I clutch her arm. "But it could. Scientists are saying it could."

She fills the pan again, turns off the water, and looks at me with a tired expression. "Oh, Calli," she sighs. "I know how you worry about things like this. I'm sure the polar bears will be fine. Truthfully, honey, what can we do about it, anyway? I have too much on my plate right now to think about saving the world."

I place a couple of glasses in the sink.

"Oh, thanks," she says. "Could you get the rest of the things from the table?"

I go back to the table and gather up the silverware.

Just another normal day in the life of the Gold family.

Why'd You Pick Me?

I am sitting with Wanda and Claire at our usual lunch table the next day when Tanya Timley strolls by.

"Look at her! She's wearing a bra!" Wanda whispers.

"Who?" I ask.

Wanda tips her head in Tanya's direction.

"Really?" I say. "How do you know?"

"You can see it," Claire says matter-of-factly, taking a bite of her peanut-butter-with-no-jelly sandwich. "Look at the back of her shirt."

I peer over at Tanya, who is in line at the salad bar. If anything's there, I can't detect it. All I notice is that the front of her shirt says WONDER GIRL in shiny gold letters.

"You have to look up close," Wanda informs me. "She doesn't even need one, anyway. She's just wearing it to be cool and act like she's so grown-up." Wanda sighs and glances down at her chest. "I asked my mother for a bra, but she said all I have is baby fat."

Claire and I don't say anything, because this is probably true. Wanda is a little on the chubby side. Claire is skinny as a stick and I am somewhere in between. I guess you could call me average in that area too.

Tanya drifts past our table with her plate of salad. She's taller than any other girl in our grade and she wears a different-colored headband every single day. She tells people it's her signature look. She has one to match every outfit, and somehow, they all look good with her fiery long red hair.

"How come all she eats is salad?" I ask Wanda and Claire. "You'd think she'd want a bag of chips once in a while."

Claire, who pretty much has an answer for everything, says, "I'm sure the modeling agency tells her what she can and can't eat."

Everyone knows that Tanya Timley models and in her spare time attends fifth grade at Southbrook Elementary.

Claire motions for the two of us to lean toward her. "I heard Tanya say that she's up for some big TV commercial," she whispers.

"Well, good for her," Wanda scoffs.

"What's the commercial for?" I ask.

"Toothpaste," Claire replies.

"How do you know?" Wanda questions.

Claire shrugs. "She sits in front of me in math."

Wanda makes a face and sticks her tongue out. Then she holds up an invisible tube of toothpaste and smiles insanely from ear to ear. "I'm Tanya Timley," she drawls. "The only toothpaste I use is for people who are better than everyone else."

Claire and I giggle as Wanda stays frozen in her ridiculous smile.

When we settle down, I glance across the cafeteria at Tanya, who is sitting with a few other fifth-grade girls. All of them are eating only salad. Becca has started eating salad a lot lately too, and I wonder if they know something I don't. Is there an unwritten rule that girls are supposed to start eating salad at a certain point? I hope not, because I don't even like salad.

A few minutes later, the lunch lady comes over to our table with her spray bottle. "Almost cleanup time," she warns. "Move it along, girls." She aims the spray toward the middle of our table and some droplets land right on Claire's sandwich.

"Well, I guess I'm done with that," Claire mutters under her breath, and glares at the lunch lady.

Wanda zips her lunch bag. "The bell's about to ring anyway," she says to Claire.

As the lunch lady begins to wipe off our table, we crumple up our garbage, toss our water bottles into the recycling bin, and walk toward the door of the cafeteria. Luckily, this year, Wanda, Claire, and I are all in the same class.

We stop at our lockers. Wanda and I share one. When I open it, Wanda checks her braces in our little mirror like she always does after lunch. "I have a piece of apple stuck in there," she wails, trying to pick it out with her fingers.

"Wanda!" Claire whispers. "Do you have to do that in front of everyone?"

"What?" Wanda says innocently.

Claire shakes her head and slams her locker door. Wanda shrugs at me.

Before we enter the room, I know that Mrs. Lamont has taken her shoes off. The smell of her feet drifts out into the hallway. She says she does that in the afternoons because her shoes start to get tight and her toes need to breathe. I guess this makes sense, but honestly, she could use some foot deodorant. One of the boys once put a little jar of foot powder on her desk, but she didn't seem to get the hint. She just raised it in the air and asked, "Who does this belong to?"

Claire, Wanda, and I all pinch our noses as we slide into our seats. Today Mrs. Lamont's socks have yellow bumblebees on them. Yesterday it was ladybugs. I'm not sure why she likes to have insects decorating her feet, but some people are just weird about certain things.

"Take your seats, boys and girls." Mrs. Lamont motions to the desks, smiling broadly. "I have a big surprise to announce."

Tanya is in our class this year too. Her seat is right next to mine. She pretty much towers over me. I check the back of her shirt, but I still can't see anything. Tanya folds her hands across the top of her desk and sits up very straight. She makes me realize that I'm slouching, so I try to sit up straight too.

Mrs. Lamont walks over to the board and writes *Peer Helper Program* in huge letters. Then she twirls around, clasps her hands, and grins. "For years," she says, "I have been trying to implement my idea for a peer program in this school, and I'm thrilled to tell you that the principal has finally given me the go-ahead."

Mrs. Lamont strolls down the middle aisle between our desks. When she passes by, Wanda fans the air in front of her face. I have to bite my lip to keep from laughing.

"Educational research has shown that when students of different ages work together, the benefits are great for both," Mrs. Lamont explains. "The older students mentor the younger ones, which helps them learn to become leaders, and the younger students also teach their peers something in return."

"What's she talking about?" I hear one of the boys say.

"Shhh," Claire whispers.

Wanda raises her hand, and Mrs. Lamont says, "Yes?"

"Exactly what is a peer, anyway?" Wanda asks.

"Well," Mrs. Lamont says. "Good question. A peer is a colleague, a coworker, a contemporary . . . Really, a peer is simply a friend." She glances around the classroom. "I think you'll all be excited about this once you understand what it is."

"Okay, but does it mean more homework?" Jason interrupts.

"No," Mrs. Lamont says. "Our class will meet once a week with the second graders in Mrs. Bezner's class to form relationships, read, help with classwork, and perhaps join together for a special project in the future. So, right now, what I'd like you to do is pull out the spirals I asked you to bring today."

I let out a small gasp as all the other kids in the room reach inside their desks for their shiny, unwritten-on, brand-new spiral notebooks. My shoulders drop as I think of Mom rushing around with all those Post-its attached to her steering wheel. Claire sees me and mouths, "Did you forget?" I nod.

These are the times when I love Claire. She pulls a spiral out of her desk like a magician and passes it down to me. "I bought some extras at the beginning of the year," Claire whispers, and I mouth, "Thanks."

Mrs. Lamont starts explaining about the Peer Helper Program, or PHP. Most of the kids are making notes in their spirals, but although I've opened mine to the first page, I'm not sure what I should be writing down. As Mrs. Lamont keeps talking, my mind drifts and I look out the window and watch leaves flutter from the trees one after the other, as if each one knows exactly the right time to fall. Does the tree or the leaf let go first?

All of a sudden, everyone is standing up and getting into a line.

"Where are we going?" I ask Claire.

"Weren't you listening?" She frowns at me.

"I sort of stopped paying attention."

"We're going up to the second-grade classroom for the first PHP get-together," Claire says importantly. "We'll be matched up with our partners. I hope I get a second grader who can at least spell."

"What do you mean, partners?" I ask Claire, following her in line.

She looks a little annoyed. "Mrs. Lamont said each of us will have our own second-grade peer, you know, one-on-one. That's how the PHP works."

"Oh," I reply. "Of course."

When we pile inside Mrs. Bezner's second-grade room, she tells us how happy she is that we will be working with her students. "We think you will find this program to be a wonderfully rewarding experience," she adds, and Mrs. Lamont nods enthusiastically.

"Now, before we choose our peers," Mrs. Bezner says, "does anyone already know someone in my class?"

Tanya Timley shoots her hand into the air.

"Yes?" Mrs. Bezner asks.

Tanya waves to a girl with long, straight blond hair and

enormous round blue eyes. "That's my cousin Ashley," Tanya says. "Ash and me. PHP. It can't be any other way."

"I guess that's all right," Mrs. Bezner says. "Okay with you, Lucy?"

"I don't see any harm," Mrs. Lamont says.

Tanya raises her hand again. "I do have a mini problem, though. I'm out of school a lot, modeling and going on auditions." Tanya bats her eyelashes and shows off her evenly spaced, very white teeth, perfect for a toothpaste commercial. "So, who will be with Ashley when I'm not here?"

"I'm sure we can work it out, Tanya," Mrs. Lamont says briskly. "Let's move on."

For the rest of the peer partners, Mrs. Bezner explains, we will be pulling numbers from a cup, and so will the second graders. The students with matching numbers will be each other's peer helpers. "I think that's the fairest way," she adds.

Mrs. Bezner is shaking one cup, and Mrs. Lamont is shaking the other, when I cannot believe what I see at the very back of the room: someone with messy light brown spiky hair, slumped over on a desk, wearing a dark blue winter jacket.

Noah Zullo?

I lean over, trying to see if it's him. I examine the jacket intently, and I'm positive it's the same one from the rink yesterday.

My hand flies up in the air, as if I am not in control

of it. "Mrs. Lamont," I hear myself saying, "I know someone too."

"You do, dear?" she says. "Who?"

"That kid over there." I point.

Several of the second graders turn to stare at the back of the room as Noah Zullo slowly raises his head and squints at me through his glasses. His skin is very pale, like a white seashell.

"I'd like to be Noah's peer," I say with a gulp. From the corner of my eye, I glimpse a confused look on Wanda's face.

"Oh, wonderful!" Mrs. Bezner replies. "Noah is new to our classroom. His family just moved here. How do you know each other?" she asks me.

I suddenly feel panicky, like Noah will blurt out that we really don't know each other and I am lying. But somehow, as I watch him blinking at me, I know he won't do that.

"We met yesterday," I say. "At the skating rink."

"Okay, then." Mrs. Bezner resumes shaking the cup with the numbers.

I smile at Noah, but he just looks at me blankly.

"Now," Mrs. Lamont says after all the numbers have been chosen. "Go ahead and find your peers. We'll have a few minutes for you to get acquainted, and then we will get together again next week for our first real PHP time."

Tanya brushes past me. "Leave it to Calli Gold to pick the weirdest kid in the entire second grade," she says. Her cousin Ashley giggles and covers her mouth. The two of them put their heads together and arms around each other in a private huddle.

Ever since Tanya called me puny last year, she and I haven't exactly liked each other very much. It's true I have been in the front row every year for class pictures, so maybe I am a little on the short side. But still, I wouldn't go around calling Tanya Timley freakishly tall, even if she is.

I stop right in front of Noah, look at him, and wonder what I've gotten myself into. My heart thumps as loudly as a basketball on a gym floor.

"Hi," I say brightly. "Remember me?"

He stares at me, with that messy hair and pale face and blank expression; then he starts wringing his hands together as if he's washing them with soap and water. Finally, with what seems like a tremendous effort, he places his hands on top of his desk and makes two tight little fists. After a moment, he looks up at me through his glasses with an almost suspicious expression.

"Why'd you pick me?" he asks.

I look around the room at the groups of fifth graders and second graders, some talking, some smiling, some seeming awkward. Ashley and Tanya are hugging each other, practically exploding with excitement. Then I look back at Noah. I don't have an answer.

Grandma Gold

𝕴'm a walker. My house is right over the small hill behind the school, at the end of the block. When I get home this afternoon, it's Grandma Gold who greets me, not Mom.

"What are you doing here?" I ask, dropping my backpack on the kitchen floor. I glance at the Calendar and the flurry of Post-it notes, wondering if I've forgotten something.

She closes the newspaper and folds her arms across her plump chest. "Now, is that any way to say hello to your favorite grandparent?" she asks, motioning me toward her for a hug.

Grandma Gold is my only grandma, since the other one died before I was born, and my grandpas are both long gone too. So technically, she has to be my favorite. There's no contest.

"I only meant, where's Mom?" I say as she wraps her fleshy arms around me. When Grandma Gold hugs me, she squeezes me right down to my lungs, so I can't get a good breath. Plus she always wears big metal necklaces and they press sharply into my chest.

"I'm here to watch you while she took your sister for an X-ray on her ankle," Grandma Gold informs me. "That sister of yours kept insisting she needed crutches, so now your mother's all worked up. Lucky I'm so close by, I ran right over."

Grandma Gold lives in a senior citizen building about a half hour away from Southbrook.

She grins at me. "It's just you and me for now, cookie. You know how long it takes at those godforsaken emergency rooms."

"Oh," I reply, even though I really want to remind her that I do not need to be watched. Do they think I'm going to run to the stove, turn on the dial, and burn the house down? Or open the window in my bedroom and jump out, just for fun?

"So, whaddya say, how about a game of Scrabble?" she proposes, winking an eye heavily coated with violet shadow. "You been practicing?"

Grandma's talent is Scrabble. She brags that she once used all her letters in two separate words in the same game. Dad says it was only one word, but she insists it was two. They got into a big argument about it, and now Dad won't play Scrabble with her anymore.

"Well," I say hesitantly, "I do have some homework."

"Oh, homework, schmomework." She waves her hand in the air. "I always say you learn more about life outside of school. I'm sure you have time for one little game. C'mon, get the board."

There's no saying no to Grandma. She doesn't give up. When I walk back into the kitchen with the Scrabble box, she's pulled out her lipstick and mirror. I'm not sure why she needs to put on lipstick to play Scrabble, but even so, while I'm setting up, she slathers on a few layers of glossy red.

"There," she says, smacking her lips. "Cookie, let me share something with you. I'm going to tell you my motto of life."

"Your motto?" I ask.

"Yeah," she says. "You know, my guiding principle."

"Okay. What is it?"

"Speak loudly and carry a red lipstick." Her mouth spreads into a wide grin; then she bursts into laughter and slaps her leg several times.

"I don't get it," I say when she quiets down.

"What do you mean you don't get it?" she snaps. "You haven't heard of Teddy Roosevelt?"

"I've heard of him."

"Don't you know he was famous for saying 'Speak softly and carry a big stick'?"

47

"No."

"See, that's what I mean," she says. "What do they teach you these days in school?"

"I think we learn that in junior high," I tell her.

"Carry a big stick . . . carry a red lipstick." She raises her eyebrows. "Oh, forget it. Pick your letters."

I reach for the bag of letters and pull out all vowels. Grandma's first word is "flower." "Six letters," she mutters. "Couldn't have gotten an 's,' now, could I? Would've been an extra fifty points right off the bat."

I make the word "are," building on her "r."

"That's all you've got?" she says, shaking her head. Her long beaded earrings swing back and forth.

She places some letters on the board and makes another long word, then tallies up the score so far. "Now, my Joel, he plays a mean game of Scrabble," she says. "Beat the pants off me once, and I think he was only fourteen at the time."

"Do you ever talk to Uncle Joel?" I ask.

"Oh, sure, all the time. He calls me from that convertible of his. Of course I can't hear a thing he's saying with all that wind in the background. Your turn."

"Can I get a snack first?"

"Fine, but not something messy," she says. Grandma Gold doesn't like it when crumbs get on the board and the letters.

After a few more words (big ones from her, little ones

from me), she grabs her purse. "I have to go out to my car for a minute," she says. "I'll be right back."

I can pretty much guess what she's doing, so she doesn't have to pretend. I know she's going out for a cigarette. Grandma Gold swears she quit smoking years ago, but we all know she sneaks one whenever she gets the craving.

Sure enough, when I peek out the front window, there she is in her car, puffing away. I'm sure there is a mark from her red lipstick on the white end of the cigarette.

This makes me think about what she said her life motto is—speak loudly and carry a red lipstick—and I realize that Dad has the same motto. The part about speaking loudly, not about carrying the red lipstick. And as I'm standing there, this timid little voice somewhere inside me asks . . . Why? Why do you need to speak loudly? If you speak quietly but have something important to say, won't people still listen?

The little voice melts away, though, when I trudge back to the kitchen table and realize how badly I'm playing. Now I have all consonants. Peering over at Grandma's letters, I see that she already has the word "night" spelled out on her rack. A lot of points.

I wait and wait. She's taking an awful long time. She must be having a second cigarette.

Suddenly, a terrible thought jumps into my head. I could switch my letters, couldn't I? She wouldn't know. If

I just had one or two vowels, then I could make a word, at least. Maybe a high-scoring word that Grandma Gold could brag about to Dad. I could quickly dump my seven letters back into the bag and pull out seven new ones and no one would know. Well, no one except me.

I start to feel the way I do when Dad goes around the dinner table and asks us for our daily accomplishments—hot and sweaty, with a mouth so dry it seems like I can't speak or breathe.

I reach for the bag of letters and hold it in my hand and swallow several times.

Just when I'm about to plunge my hand inside, I hear the front door open. I toss the bag back into the middle of the table and quickly start shuffling the letters on my rack.

"Okeydokey," Grandma says, coming into the kitchen with a burst of cool air. "I'm ready." Her breath stinks. "I think it was your turn."

"Yeah," I say, my voice coming out a little shaky.

"You got anything?" she asks.

I look down at my letters and it hits me: I really was going to cheat. I really was going to do it. If Grandma hadn't come barreling through the door at that very moment, I would have. I bite my lip. On how many occasions has Dad hammered in his belief about turning tough times into triumph? How you never give up, or give in, and all that stuff. Alex does it in basketball games, and Becca in skating. Me? I was ready to crumble within minutes, over a dumb Scrabble game. Maybe I should change my last name.

"Need any help?" Grandma Gold asks.

"No," I say sullenly.

Now not only do I have the guilt of knowing how easily I would have cheated, but I'm also stuck with the letters I picked.

Like today, when Noah asked me why I picked him.

At first, I didn't say anything. Why did I pick him?

I thought about it for a minute; then I simply told him, "Because I did."

He stared at me, his mouth a bright small circle. Then, in a tiny squeaky voice, he said, "So now you're stuck with me."

What things to be stuck with. All consonants and Noah Zullo.

Improv?

Becca's ankle turns out to be fine, and Mom is completely aggravated about wasting three hours getting it X-rayed. She's slapping things around the kitchen, grumbling about being off schedule, and muttering how she didn't get anything done this afternoon. We all know that when she gets like this, it's best to stay out of her way.

Grandma left in a rush, refusing the offer to stay for dinner. "I have just enough time to get to my Zumba class," she said as she hurried out.

At dinnertime, like usual, Dad asks Alex for his accomplishment of the day, and Becca for hers. I'm barely listening. I'm pushing my corn around on my plate, creating a pathway for the broccoli to wade through, when

Dad calls out, "Calli! I had a brainstorm today, and it concerns you!"

"A brainstorm?" I repeat, dropping my fork. "What do you mean, a brainstorm?"

"Now, don't say anything right away," he tells me, smiling broadly. "Just hear me out first, okay?"

"Okay," I say hesitantly.

"Are you ready?"

"Yeah."

"You're sure?"

"Yeah, Dad, I'm ready."

He sits back in his chair and clasps his hands together. "Okay." He pauses dramatically. "Improv."

"Improv?" I echo.

"Bingo."

Becca snorts before I have a chance to react. "You're not saying you think Calli should try acting now, are you?"

He nods. "That's exactly what I'm saying."

"Acting?" I scrunch up my nose and shake my head. "Dad . . ."

"Consider it, Calli," he says. "You've always had a terrific imagination. You think so much about all the characters in the books you read. Some of the world's greatest actors are really shy people inside, you know."

My heart flutters. "You think I'm shy?"

"Well," he says, chuckling, "I suppose it's no secret you're a little quieter than the rest of us."

"I guess," I answer softly.

My hands fall to my lap as I try to imagine what an improv class would be like. People pretending to be animals, slithering around the floor like snakes or flapping their arms like birds? Or making up skits and telling really funny jokes? Or imitating famous people while everyone else has to guess who they are?

"I don't know, Dad," I say, swallowing the lump in my throat.

"You know what your father always promotes," Mom pipes up.

I recite it in a bored-sounding voice. "'Try anything once,' I know."

"Hey, you could move to Hollywood, Cal," Alex offers, grinning at me. "Ride around in a limo and go to lots of cool parties."

Becca snorts again.

"Look," Dad says. "All I'm asking is that you give it a shot. You know, your aunt Marjorie had a little stint in the theater . . . before she went crazy and ran off to New Zealand, that is."

"She did?" Aunt Marjorie is my dad's younger sister. I've never met her. She lives farther away than Uncle Joel. Grandma Gold says something went wrong with her but it certainly isn't *her* fault that Marjorie turned out to be a lunatic.

"She acted in college," Dad says, nodding. "Even had the lead in one of the big plays. Had such a bright future

ahead of her. Agents were calling. I never could understand why she did what she did." He raises his eyebrows.
"Maybe you take after her."

"Okay, Dad, I'll think about it," I say. Then it dawns
on me that he is comparing me to the relative in our family who is known as offbeat and bizarre, the one who
everyone says marches to a different drummer. The one
who wants nothing to do with anyone else.

"Good girl. You give it some thought." Dad reaches
into his shirt pocket. "Here's a little brochure you can
read over." He claps a hand to his forehead. "I don't know
why I didn't think of this before."

I glance at the title of the brochure, which asks: *Have
you always wanted to be on the stage?* and my immediate
reaction is no. Never. Not even once.

Dad bolts up from his chair, sticks one arm out and
puts the other hand across his chest. "'To be, or not to
be,'" he croons with a British accent. "'That is the question.'"

"What are you doing?" Becca says, rolling her eyes.

"I'm demonstrating a little Shakespeare for my soon-
to-be-actress daughter." He beams at me. Then he closes
one eye, stretches his arms forward, and positions his
hands into a frame. "I can picture the Academy Award
now."

I look back at the brochure, which shows a group of
people wearing black turtlenecks. *Let us bring out your
inner muse,* it states.

All I can think is what is a muse? And do I want to bring mine out?

I slide the brochure into the back pocket of my jeans as Dad sits down in his chair and winks at me. "This could be it," he says, nodding. "This could be your passion."

My passion, I think.

Improv?

Maybe . . .

Mom is starting to clear the dinner dishes when I see that Alex and Becca have conveniently left the kitchen again. With one more wink at me, Dad grabs his phone from the counter and says he needs to pick up his messages.

I look at Mom. "I have homework," I inform her. "I didn't get it done after school because Grandma Gold was here. She made me play Scrabble with her."

"Oh, fine," she sighs, pushing her hair back from her forehead. "I guess it's just me and this big mess."

I feel bad when I see the pile of dirty dishes stacked by the sink. "Do you want me to help you?" I ask.

She doesn't answer right away. She looks a little sad. Then her voice comes out kind of dreamy-sounding. "I read somewhere that the average mother washes something like one hundred thousand dishes in her life," she says. "Or was it three hundred thousand?" Her shoulders sag. "I can't remember."

"Wow," I say. "Either way, that's a lot of dishes. . . . Mom, I'll help you. I don't have that much homework."

"No, no, it's okay." She gives me a weak smile. "Go on. I'm fine." She looks away from me and turns on the water at the sink.

I take a last glance at her, drag my backpack up to my room, park it on the floor, and pull out the sheet of math problems due tomorrow. Before I start, I look around my room. You could say that it is in a state of transition right now. I have Becca's old furniture, because she is redoing her room so it can be a teenage hangout kind of place. Mom is letting her order lots of new things from a Web site. She says I can do that too when I'm thirteen, but for now, it's fine for me to use Becca's old dresser and desk. With my old bed and curtains. And a bookshelf that Alex wasn't using anymore. Claire describes the look of my room as "unique," but I know that's just a nice way of saying nothing matches and it doesn't make any sense.

I start working on the first math problem when I remember the improv brochure. I pull it out of my pocket and examine the people on the front in their snug black turtlenecks. The background is black too, so it almost looks like their heads are floating in space. Maybe they want it to look that way.

I go into my closet, remembering that I have a long-sleeved black shirt. I pull it from the hanger, slide it over the shirt I'm wearing, then look at myself in the mirror on the back of the closet door. I hold up the brochure next to my face. Do I look like an improv person? Is this "it," like Dad said?

The girl I see in the mirror just looks like the same old me, except in a black shirt. In-between hair—not really curly or straight, but sort of wavy. Brown eyes, a random freckle in the middle of my cheek, and a pretty good smile. Not extraordinarily beautiful, but not ugly either. Average, I guess.

Suddenly, there's a knock on my bedroom door. I rip off the black shirt and toss it, along with the improv brochure, into my closet and quickly shut the door.

Mom comes in holding a stack of folded laundry and places it on my bed. Her face looks a little droopy and tired but not quite as sad as before. She takes off her glasses, cleans them on the edge of her sweater, then puts them back on. "So how's the homework going?" she asks.

"Fine, I guess."

She glances at my worksheet. "What are you working on?"

"Math."

"Can't help you there." She smiles. "That's Dad's department."

"I don't really need help, but thanks anyway." I worry she's going to open my closet door and see that I threw the improv brochure and the black shirt on the floor.

Instead, she sighs and glances out my window at the shadowy sky. She goes to the window, pulls down the blinds, then pauses near the dresser. "It gets dark so early this time of year." She shakes her head and reaches for my T-shirts, neatly folded on top of the laundry stack.

"I'll just be a few minutes," she tells me. "I want to get these clothes put away. Then you can get back to your homework."

"It's okay," I say.

She opens a dresser drawer and lays the T-shirts inside, then opens another and puts in several pairs of rolled-up socks.

"Mom?" I ask.

"Mmm?" she replies, closing the sock drawer.

"How come Dad never talks to Aunt Marjorie or Uncle Joel?"

"Well," she says, shrugging, "siblings sometimes don't stay as close when they get older and have their own lives and families. I try to keep in touch with my brother, but we're both so busy."

I think about that for a minute. "Claire's mom sees her sister all the time."

"She lives right here in Southbrook, though. It's harder to stay close when you all live in different cities."

"Oh," I say. I want to ask her if Aunt Marjorie's really a lunatic, like Grandma Gold claims, but she picks up a pair of jeans and says, "These are Becca's. Bring them to her room for me, would you?"

As I trudge down the hall toward my sister's room, I'm prepared for a closed door and her irritated voice when I knock, but instead, her door is open and she's not in there. I lay the jeans on her bed, then hear a chirp from her computer. A message pops up on her screen from

Tay412, who I know is her friend Taylor from the Synchronettes. *What happened with Ruthless?* the message says.

About one second after I've read the message, Becca storms into her room. "What are you doing in here?" she shrieks. "Get out of my room. Are you spying on me?" She bolts over to her computer and turns off the screen.

"I wasn't spying on you," I answer. "Mom sent me in with your jeans." I point to the bed.

"So why were you looking at my computer?" she demands, hands on her hips.

"I w-wasn't . . . ," I stutter.

Becca flips her hair and flings a hand at me. "You can leave now."

When I return to my room, Mom has finished putting away my laundry but she's sitting on my bed. She looks at me vacantly, like she forgot where she was. Then she puts her hands on either side of her and pushes herself up. "See, this is why I never sit down during the day," she says, laughing. "Once I do, I can't get up, and I still have so much more to do tonight."

She absentmindedly picks up a photograph from my dresser, then puts it down. "Okay," she says, clapping her hands. "Enough time-wasting. You get back to your homework, and I'll get back to my never-ending goal of keeping this house in order."

When she leaves, I glance at the photograph she picked up. The picture is of the five of us, last year on Mom's birthday. I remember that Grandma Gold took it. I've heard people say you can tell a lot from a photograph, and I see how true that is.

We're all around the kitchen table. Becca had just come from skating, so she is standing right in front, in her bright purple velour practice dress. For some reason, she draped one of her skating medals around her neck. Alex is in his basketball uniform, and my dad is in his tie and white shirt. They're on either side of Mom, who is showing off her cake. Everyone is smiling. Everyone except me, that is. I'm on the other side of Dad, sort of tucked behind him, and the only parts of me that are visible are half of my face, a shoulder, and an arm. I never realized it before, but it looks like I'm not really part of the picture.

It looks like I'm hiding.

I gather up the shirt from my closet floor and try to imagine myself wearing it in the family photo. Would the whole of me be showing if I was a successful improv star, proudly posing along with the rest of them?

My shoulders drop and I go back to my closet, hang up the shirt, then bury the brochure in my underwear drawer. I pull the big Webster's dictionary from my bookshelf and look up the word "muse," which, it turns out, is a Greek goddess and also a source of inspiration.

I doubt that the improv place is where I will find inspiration, but if I know Dad, he's not going to let it go until I give it a try.

I start again on the first math problems, then stop with my pencil in midair and look back at the family photo. What did Dad say before, in the kitchen? *To be, or not to be, that is the question.* . . .

But the real question, I realize, is why must I *do* something to *be* somebody in this family?

Peer Helper Problems

The next week, as my class is walking down the hallway toward the second-grade rooms for our first real
PHP time, my stomach feels all jumbled and nervous.
Picking Noah really was such a dumb move. He's weird,
doesn't talk much, and obviously has some issues. What
was I thinking?

When we get to Mrs. Bezner's room, most of the kids
wave or shout hi to their peers, who wave excitedly and
shout back in return. I spot Noah sitting at his desk. He
isn't covering up his face this time, though; he's actually
looking toward the doorway. He seems a little . . . hope-
ful. But when he sees me, he quickly drops his head
onto the desk and pulls both of his arms around it. His
hair looks the same, like it's never been combed in his
entire life.

"Today," Mrs. Bezner announces as the fifth graders line up on one side of the room, "we decided a nice way to start our Peer Helper Program would be to have the peer teams choose a book to read together, and then discuss the story and how it relates to your own life experiences. See if you can discover some things you have in common with each other." She gestures to a bookcase at the back of the room. "Fifth graders, go ahead and find your peers, and then why don't we have this side of the room go to the bookcase first." She points to the side of the classroom that doesn't include Noah.

The fifth graders start making their way to their second-grade partners. As I approach Noah, I try to act confident, and paste a big smile on my face, just in case anyone looks at me. I take a seat at an empty desk next to him. I notice that he's not wearing his jacket today. He has an itchy-looking green sweater on. He doesn't acknowledge me at all.

"Hi." I tip my head toward him. "Me again."

Noah doesn't answer, so I continue. "We've never officially met. My name's Calli, and yours is . . . ?"

Finally, he turns and glances at me distrustfully through his glasses, which look dirty. They're sitting crookedly on his nose so only one eyebrow is showing.

"Noah," I state. "Right? So, Noah . . . what kinds of books do you like to read?"

He frowns and scrunches his mouth up. "I'm not good at reading."

I'm so surprised he answered me that I stare at him. He turns away and crosses his arms like I made him mad.

"That's okay," I say quickly. "I can read to you."

He gives a little shrug.

Mrs. Bezner tells the rest of us to go to the bookcase.

"Should we go over and choose a book?" I ask, scooting my chair closer to him.

Noah shrugs again; then he mumbles, "You know what else? I can't make stuff."

"Like art projects, you mean?"

He nods in a jerky sort of way.

"Why not?" I ask.

"I'm not good at that."

"So." I rest my chin on my hand and tap my cheek. "You're not good at reading, and you're not good at making stuff."

"Yeah." His hands are shaking a bit and he starts wringing them again, like he did the day I asked to be his peer helper.

"Well." I try jabbing him lightly with my elbow, like I'm joking. "There must be something you're good at."

"There isn't," Noah Zullo says, and in one quick motion, he darts under his desk.

"Noah?" I peek under the desk. I guess he didn't think my joke was funny.

"I don't need a peer helper," he croaks, and wraps his arms around his knees. "Leave me alone."

I pull myself back up and glance around the room. No

one seems to realize that Noah is under his desk and I am now sitting by myself. We never even got a book. Claire has a very serious look on her face while she is listening to her peer, a small boy with a buttoned-up blue shirt like Dad wears to work. Wanda and her peer, a girl with a frizzy ponytail, are whispering to each other. Tanya is turning the pages of a book while Ashley is snuggled next to her. The two of them are wearing matching pink headbands.

"Is everything all right?"

I look up to see Mrs. Bezner standing over me. She bends down and spots Noah, who scoots backward so he's even farther underneath the desk.

Mrs. Bezner gives me a kind smile. "Noah's been having some trouble adjusting," she confides in a low voice. "Do you think you'll be able to work with him?"

I feel a small hand wrap itself around my ankle. Not angrily or tightly, just sort of like it's looking for something to hold on to.

Mrs. Bezner is waiting for my answer and that little hand is not letting go.

"Everything's fine," I tell her as I duck under the desk too. I poke my head out. "Noah and I decided that it would be more fun and private to work under his desk today."

Mrs. Bezner nods. "I don't have a problem with creative learning," she says as she walks away.

Noah lets go of my ankle as another pair of feet

approaches. These feet are wearing socks with butterflies on them. Mrs. Lamont. I point to the socks, then pinch my nose together with my thumb and forefinger and wave my hand in front of my face.

Noah laughs.

I let go of my nose and turn to him. "Did you just laugh?"

"No."

"I swear I heard you laugh just now."

"It's bad to swear," Noah says.

"Swear, swear, swear!"

As a second laugh erupts from Noah, my heart feels all full and bursting and good.

I'm about to tell Noah about Mrs. Lamont and her insect socks but he stops laughing and a shadow crosses his face. He turns away from me and pulls at a thread that dangles from the front of his sweater. He gives the thread a fierce tug, rips it off, and winds it tightly around his finger. The tip of his finger starts to turn red.

The two of us sit in silence as he wraps and unwraps the thread. I glance around in the dim space under the desk and spot a chewed-up pencil on the floor behind Noah. Pairs of shoes scurry past and bits of conversation drift down from above. Then Mrs. Lamont announces, "Five more minutes, everyone."

I let out a sigh. "We never read a book like we were supposed to today, did we?"

Noah unwinds the thread, sticks it back on the front

of his sweater, and puts his arms around his knees again. "I don't care," he mumbles. "I don't care about reading books, or peer helpers, because they're dumb and stupid."

"Why?"

"Just because."

I want to reach out and smooth down his spiky, messy hair, but instead, I ease myself out from under the desk and join the rest of my class.

As the fifth graders file out of the room, Wanda and Claire turn to me.

"Mine is just the cutest little girl you ever saw," Wanda says.

"I feel so important," Claire confides. "So . . . mature."

Tanya is taking long strides with her long legs, and I hear her brag that if there is a peer helper award at the end of this program, she and Ashley will surely receive it, because they're "so connected."

I'm even more quiet than usual. I don't feel mature or connected or anything except worried.

9

Okay, Muse, I'm Ready

I really do love that I'm a walker. Walking home gives me time to think, even if it's only for a few minutes. Besides when I'm sleeping, this is just about the only part of the day that I'm by myself. I'm nervous about next year, when I'll take the bus to junior high. The bus always seems so crowded and noisy and crazy. Kind of like my family. I doubt I'll be able to get much thinking done on the bus.

What I think about on my way home is Noah. I wonder why he is the way he is and if this peer helper thing is going to work out. With what happened today, I don't know how it possibly can. Should I talk to Mrs. Lamont before the next PHP time? Or maybe I should talk to Mrs. Bezner. I have an awful feeling that this is going to turn out like my attempts at gymnastics and ballet and violin.

My backpack is heavy today, and I shift it to the other shoulder. If I did talk to Mrs. Lamont or Mrs. Bezner, what would I say, anyway? After all, I asked to be paired with Noah. I could have been with a normal second grader. Why did I say I knew Noah?

I let out a big sigh and kick a rock. The rock tumbles ahead of me and lands on someone's lawn. Another thing about walking: you notice things you wouldn't otherwise. As I continue down the sidewalk, I see that pretty much all the leaves are off the trees now, and there are paper bags stuffed with them in front of almost every house. Somehow this doesn't seem right. Am I the only person in Southbrook who likes fall leaves better when they're scattered on the grass? I guess people want their yards to be clean and neat now that it's November. Everyone has started saying, "Winter's just around the corner," as if there's a big snowstorm lurking on the next block.

When the wind kicks up, I'm secretly glad Mom insisted I take my warmer jacket this morning. Some houses still have their Halloween decorations up. There are a couple of houses in our neighborhood that have the skeletons and pumpkins out until practically the winter, and Mom calls those houses leavers—people who just leave stuff outside all the time, like they've forgotten about it. Mom can't stand that.

When I reach my house (our decorations are neatly packed away until next year), I shut the door behind me. "I'm home!" I call out.

Mom answers cheerfully from the kitchen, where she's sticking yellow Post-its on the Calendar. Calli-color Post-its. I drop my backpack.

"How was school?" she says brightly.

"What are you doing?" The yellow Post-its all say *Calli—Improv—4 to 5 p.m.*

She whirls around. "Guess what? I signed you up for the improv class today."

"You did?"

"Dad and I talked it over last night, Calli, and we were concerned that if we let you think about it too long, you'd never do it. We really want you to give this a try." She grins at me. "Like Dad said, this might be it! You know, your passion! Your talent!"

"But, Mom, I told Dad I would consider it. . . . I thought it was my decision."

She shrugs. "Look, honey. It's just four classes. We'd like you to give it a chance and then see what you think. The first one is next week."

Wanda always says she can tell my feelings just by looking at my face, and I know right now my face is showing a whole collection of emotions: exasperation and frustration and surprise and worry. Mom must know this about me too, because when she glances over, she suddenly gets angry.

"Now you listen to me, Calli Gold," she says, pointing at me. "You don't know how lucky you kids are. I never had any of these privileges growing up. Your dad certainly did, but I didn't have the chance to ice-skate or take dance classes or play a sport. My parents couldn't afford any of that."

I know what's coming next. The piano story.

"I showed some natural talent at the piano when I was your age, but my parents couldn't pay for lessons." Her voice cracks. "What might I have been? A concert pianist? A composer? Who knows? I never had the opportunity to find out."

She sighs. "All Dad and I want is for our children to realize their full potential. If you have a talent, it shouldn't stay hidden inside you."

"Okay, Mom." I hang my head, the most thankless child on earth. "I'll try the improv class."

"Great." She dabs at her nose. "That's the spirit."

I attempt a smile.

She finishes putting up the Post-its. "I think you're going to like it. You're going to have a lot of fun with this, I just know."

"Yeah," I answer weakly.

"So, tell me about your day," she says while shuffling through the mail.

"Well, we started this new program today. We're going to be peer helpers to one of the second-grade classes."

"How nice," she mumbles as she tears open an envelope.

I open my mouth, then close it. How can I begin to explain about choosing Noah and how he hid under his desk while all the other peer helpers read books together?

"So." She looks up. "Are you hungry?"

"Not really." I'd been planning to dig into the bag of jelly beans in the pantry (I only like the reds) but I don't feel like it anymore. "I think I'll go upstairs for a while."

"Okay," she replies. "Maybe you'll tell me more about that new helper program later?"

I shrug "It was only the first day."

I head toward the stairs. Just four classes. I can get through that, can't I?

In the upstairs hall, I pass by Alex's room, with his shiny basketball trophies, then Becca's, with her medals hanging by their colored ribbons, and walk into my mismatched bedroom. I close the door, shuffle through my underwear drawer until I find the improv brochure, then read the part about bringing out my inner muse. Muse . . . what did that word mean again? I look it up once more. A Greek goddess . . . a source of inspiration . . . Neither of those things sounds very much like me.

But then, below those meanings, I see another listing. I must have missed it before. *Muse: to ponder, consider, or deliberate at length.*

To think.

I gasp and stare at the dictionary. Maybe this *is* it. Maybe Mom and Dad are right. I love to think! I was just thinking about thinking when I was walking home!

Is that what improv is all about, really? Thinking?

For some reason, I remember that baby chick in the museum, the one huddled in its feathers, the one I wanted to comfort. Why was the chick so reluctant to join the others? Was it missing out on all the fun?

Am I?

I examine the improv people in their black turtlenecks, then pull my black shirt off the hanger. "Looks like I'm going to be wearing you," I say.

I hold up the shirt and look at myself in the mirror. What if acting really is my talent, my passion . . . and I'm the scared baby chick, not wanting to try something new and fun?

I pull the shirt over the one I'm wearing. "I'm a Gold, too," I say softly. Then I repeat, louder, "I'm a Gold, I'm a Gold, I'm a G . . ." The last one comes out as a Gulp but I swallow that right back down and put the brochure on my dresser, next to the family picture.

I take a deep breath. "Okay, muse. Whatever you are, I'm ready."

One Lone Leaf

Over the weekend, the sky stays a constant gray, and it never stops raining. Wanda calls in the early afternoon on Sunday and begs me to come over and watch a movie with her and Claire in her basement. I find Mom at her desk in the kitchen and ask if she can drive me to Wanda's house.

"I've got to get forty pairs of tights labeled," she says, holding packages of skating tights in one hand and a black Sharpie in the other. "Do me a favor, honey. Ask Dad, okay?"

"He's watching that basketball video with Alex."

"He can take a break for ten minutes," she sighs. "I have to get this done by tonight."

I find Alex and Dad on the sofa. The video is paused and Dad is talking and gesturing with the remote. "Look at his position there. They've got their defensive strategy down. You're going to need to get around number twelve."

Alex nods, plunges his hand into a box of cereal, and takes out a handful. A few pieces of cereal fall on the carpet but he doesn't notice as he stuffs his mouth.

"Dad?" I ask. "Can you drive me to Wanda's?"

"Sure," he says. "In a minute. Alex and I are in the middle of this."

I sit on the floor and wait. Dad reaches over to muss my hair like he usually does; then he hits the play button. "Alex, do you see that?"

Alex stands and tosses a lime green rubber ball into the air as if he's making a shot. "You told me before, Dad. I got it."

"Okay," Dad says, then looks over at me. "Maybe this is a good time for a break. How about if I drive Calli to her friend's house, then we'll watch the rest of this?"

Alex throws the ball in my direction. "Think fast," he shouts.

The ball plunks the side of my head. "Hey," I groan.

"Alex!" Dad says. "You all right, Calli?"

I throw the ball back at my brother, but it lands several feet away from him.

"Looks like you need some work on your passing skills," Alex says, teasing.

"C'mon, let's go," Dad says to me, jingling his keys.

I make a face at Alex, then grab my jacket and climb into the backseat of Dad's car.

Dad backs out of the garage. "Another big game next week. Alex and I are analyzing a tape of the other team."

I watch the raindrops splatter the window. "How did you get a tape of the other team?"

He grins. "I went over to their practice yesterday and just started taping. It was easy as pie. Everyone probably thought I was someone's dad." He lets out a sneaky-sounding laugh. "Little did they know I was a spy."

"Are you allowed to do that?"

"No one said I couldn't," he answers innocently. "I can't think of a better way for Alex to have an edge. Know the other team inside and out. Discover their weaknesses. That's what the pros do, you know."

"Oh."

"That way, he can anticipate their moves. His coach isn't doing stuff like that, getting the dirt on their opponents, so I am." He pulls into Wanda's driveway.

"So," he says, smiling at me, "you excited for your first improv class?"

"Yeah, Dad. I am."

"That's my girl," he says. "I'll want to hear all about it."

I nod.

He looks out the window. "It's pouring now. You want an umbrella?"

"No, I'm okay."

"Well, if Mom was here, I know she'd tell you to put on your hood, so I'll have to step in." He waggles a finger at me. "Put on your hood, honey," he says in a higher-pitched voice.

I laugh, pull up my hood, then run out into the rain. He cracks the window and shouts, "To be, or not to be!" I wave goodbye, then ring Wanda's doorbell.

Within a few minutes, Wanda, Claire, and I are snuggled in Wanda's basement with a bowl of warm, buttery popcorn, a bag of M&M'S, and one of our favorite movies.

"This is great," Wanda sighs, pulling a blanket around her. "I'm so happy you could come over. I hate this rain. I can't wait for it to snow."

Claire and I agree.

"We'll go sledding," I say.

"Of course we will." Wanda pokes me. "Like we always do."

"Be quiet. I love this part," Claire says, and we stop talking.

Wanda picks out three yellow M&M'S when the scene is over, and pops them into her mouth. "The kid in this movie," she says. "Doesn't he look like your peer? What's his name? Noah?"

With my new worry about the improv class, I'd almost forgotten about Noah. I look at the character she's talking about—a scrawny, sorry-looking boy with messy hair and a sad expression.

"You think?" I ask.

"Yeah," Wanda says. "What's up with him, anyway, Calli? Is he ADD?"

"I'm not sure."

"He does fit some of the characteristics," Claire says importantly. We both stare at her. Is there anything she doesn't get?

"Did you really know him?" Wanda asks.

"Well, sort of. I mean, I met him, but he didn't exactly meet me, I guess you could say."

"Shhh," Claire says, pointing to the TV.

"I don't think he has any friends," Wanda whispers. "He's kind of weird. I hope you can do stuff with him— you know, like all the other peer helpers."

"I guess I'll have to see what happens." I sit up, wishing that we would get off the subject of Noah. "Let's watch the movie, okay?"

Wanda picks out another bunch of M&M'S. Only orange.

"You're the weird one," I whisper to her.

She laughs. "Everyone's a little weird."

"Will you two be quiet?" Claire snaps, and Wanda says, "Okay, relax."

We settle down and turn to the TV. Wanda falls asleep halfway through and I have to wake her up when the movie ends.

We start to play cards; then Wanda's mom comes down to the basement. "Calli, your mom is waiting out front. She's honking the horn pretty loudly."

When I run from Wanda's front door to Mom's van, the rain is so heavy that my jacket and jeans get soaked. Alex is in the front seat with his headphones on and Mom has a panicky look. She's wearing her SYNCHRONETTES MOM jacket.

"Calli," she shrieks. "Buckle up! I completely lost track of the time, and I forgot you were at Wanda's!"

"Why?" I say. "What's going on?"

"It's four-thirty! Becca's exhibition! It's at five!" She sounds a little hysterical. "I had to make the extra trip to get you, and now we're late! We'll never get a parking space!"

I reach for the seat belt and she glances back at me. "Oh, look at you, you're sopping wet. Well, I'm sorry, but there's absolutely no time for you to change. You'll just have to air-dry."

"Becca's exhibition is tonight?" I ask.

"I told you this morning," Mom shouts, careening backward out of Wanda's driveway.

"I guess I didn't hear you."

"It was on the Calendar!"

"I didn't look."

"Dad's already there with Becca," she says.

Alex is drumming his fingers on the dashboard and mouthing the words to a song.

The wipers barely keep the rain cleared from the window. A few minutes later, Mom turns into the rink. "The parking lot is jammed. It's a madhouse, like usual."

Before Becca's skating team begins its competition season, the girls put on a show for their families and friends. All the other skating teams from the rink are in the show too. It's a big deal. Everyone comes.

Mom veers into the last space in the far parking lot, then gets out, whips open an umbrella, and puts her arm around me. We run through the rain toward the door of the rink. Alex ambles behind like it's not even raining. "Find us when you get inside," Mom calls back.

At the rink, Mom stops just inside the door, shakes out the umbrella, then closes it. Another Synchronettes mom spots her. "Karen," the other mom yells. "We've got hairpiece trouble! Three of them fell out during warm-ups! If that happens in a competition, we're dead!"

The two of them start talking about what they can do to make the skaters' hairpieces stay in place. Mom is suggesting clips and bobby pins and barrettes, but the other mom keeps insisting they need to use a special type of glue. The doors to the rink open, and Alex walks in, his hair dripping water.

This is the weirdest thing of the day. Just before the rink doors close, somehow, through the downpour, I catch sight of a very small tree in the parking lot with one single leaf clinging to a skinny branch. The leaf is hanging there, sort of fragile, not another leaf in sight anywhere on the whole tree.

That leaf makes me think of all those paper bags stuffed with leaves, and then, for some reason, of Noah, and how he dove under his desk and grabbed my ankle when Mrs. Bezner came by. The leaf is holding on to the tree in the same way that Noah was holding on to my ankle.

He was holding on to *me*.

"C'mon, Calli," Mom says. "They're saving seats for us."

As Mom tugs on my arm, I glance at the lone leaf and realize I was able to make Noah laugh. I remember the sound—jingly and light and clear, but also unsure, like he was out of practice. When he was laughing, he didn't look so different. He covered his mouth with his hand and threw his head back. His eyes crinkled up into two lines behind his glasses. He looked like a normal kid.

I decide right then and there that I'm not saying anything to Mrs. Lamont or Mrs. Bezner. I picked Noah, and I'm sticking it out.

Becca's Lie

*G*randma Gold and Dad are holding part of a row in the stands with Grandma's purse and Dad's shoes used as seat-savers. "People are getting vicious," Dad reports. "Fifty times, someone tried to take these seats."

Grandma gives me one of her lung-crushing hugs. "How are you, Calli-beans?" she says, but doesn't listen for my reply. "I'm freezing. Can't they turn the heat on with all these people here?"

"There are warmers, Mother." Dad points to the ceiling.

"They're not doing very much good," she snaps. "I should have brought a blanket. Or a comforter!"

"Becca's team is on first," Mom says, consulting the program. Then she scans the rink. "Where's Alex?"

"I see him," I say, and Mom asks, "Where?"

I point to Alex, who's leaning against a wall by the skaters' dressing rooms, with his headphones still on.

"Oh, fine," she says. "We don't really have room for him anyway."

I am squeezed between Mom and Grandma Gold. My jeans are still wet and now plastered to my legs, but I don't say anything. Neither of my parents would hear me anyway, because Becca is about to skate.

The skaters on Becca's team are wearing their costumes from last year. They are supposed to look like bikinis, with a piece of skin-colored fabric between the top and bottom. It looks fake. So does their hair, because every skater has the same curly ponytail attached to their real hair. Their makeup is exactly the same too. They look like identical dolls in a row on a store shelf.

Dad stares straight ahead, focusing only on Becca. As they begin their routine, Grandma Gold hisses loudly, "I think I've seen this one before."

"You have," Mom whispers. "The new routine isn't perfected yet, so they decided to perform the one from last year, but they made a few changes."

"All this fuss to see something I've already seen?"

Mom shoots Grandma Gold a look, and she shoots one back. I'm in the middle of a look war. Dad doesn't notice; he's just watching Becca.

The songs for this routine are about surfers and the beach and California girls. It's supposed to be fun and happy, but I can see Coach Ruthless on the side, aggravated as usual.

The girls skate in a long line with their arms around each other, then break apart and form three circles. Then the circles magically blend together and the girls are in two lines. Becca is in the middle of the front line.

As the girls start to skate forward, one skater's hairpiece flies off, and Mom groans. "Glue," she mumbles.

"Looks like someone let their toy poodle out on the ice." Grandma Gold gestures to the curly hairpiece.

"Shhh!" Dad hisses.

"Everyone else seems to be talking," Grandma Gold points out. She's right. People all around me are chatting loudly, and I wonder why they all had to save seats for a show they're not even watching.

Becca catches her blade on the ice and stumbles. The girl next to her almost trips and jerks Becca's arm. Mom gasps, and even Dad breaks his stare for a moment. Mom holds a hand across her heart.

"She's fine," I whisper. "She didn't fall."

Mom nods nervously.

Becca's team finishes the routine and takes a bow, and then we have to sit through routines from five other teams. Alex has not moved from his spot against the wall. Finally, it dawns on me why he's standing there. He's much closer to the skaters as they go into and out of the dressing rooms. I'm not sure how he can tell what they really look like, though, with all that makeup and fake hair.

After the exhibition ends, there is a mad rush from the stands, but then everyone waits around for the skaters to come out. As each skater appears, her family screams and runs up to her and starts taking pictures. Then the skaters hug each other. Then their families hug them. Then they take more pictures.

The rink is so crowded I hardly have an inch of space. Mom is talking to the other skating moms, all of them in their Synchronettes jackets. Grandma Gold informs us she is going to the ladies' room. "Don't expect me back soon. I'm sure the line's out the door."

"Where is Becca?" Mom asks.

I spot her, but she's not making her way toward us. She's at the far end of the crowd, near a corner of the rink. "I'll be right back," I tell Mom. I weave my way through the knots of people. When I'm just a few feet from Becca, I realize she's crying. Ruthless is standing next to her, looking even more irritated than usual.

Becca says something; then I hear Ruthless say, "Look, Gold. One more mistake like that and I'm sending in the alternate. We talked about this. We can't afford errors. Not if we want to beat the Lady Reds this year." Ruthless starts to march away, then turns back. "And we will."

Becca leans against the half wall surrounding the ice

rink and covers her face with her hands. I don't think she sees me. Then she takes her hands away, wipes her eyes, and straightens her shoulders. When she reaches for her skating bag, I dash into the crowd, and I'm back with my parents before Becca finds us.

"There she is!" Dad yells out. "Great job out there. This is going to be your best season yet. I just know it. First place every time."

Becca gives him a weak smile.

"What's the matter?" he says. "Don't worry about that little slipup. Happens to even the best skaters! C'mon, how many times have you seen those top girls fall at the Olympics?"

Becca nods at Dad as he pats her on the back; then Mom snaps a picture of the two of them. "What took you so long?" she asks Becca.

"Oh, nothing," Becca answers, and waves to Taylor. "Get a picture of us," she demands, sounding like her normal self, and squeezes Taylor in a hug. My sister puts on her biggest Synchronettes smile as if nothing happened. But when they let go, another girl walks by Becca and whips her curly hairpiece around so hard that it smacks Becca in the face. I think it was the girl who was skating next to Becca when she stumbled. I hear Taylor whisper, "Just shake it off."

Mom calls out happily, "Everyone's going to the Chandelier!"

The crowd begins to move toward the doors. Grandma Gold appears and grabs my arm. "It's a stampede," she yells. "Hold on to me!"

The restaurant in Southbrook that everyone calls the Chandelier turns out to be just as packed as the skating rink. The reason people call it that is because an enormous chandelier with over one thousand tiny lightbulbs hangs in the entryway. The real name of the restaurant is Pete's Family Inn and the good thing about it is that they serve breakfast anytime.

When we're finally seated at a table, we lift our water glasses to toast Becca on a successful competition season. She's still wearing the fake ponytail but her makeup has smeared a little.

She rubs her elbow. "I think I bruised my arm."

"You're good," Dad says. "You're real good, Bec. You just shine out there."

"Yeah," she says. "That's what my coach told me after the exhibition. That's why I was late finding you . . . she talked to me afterwards. . . . She told me not to worry about losing my footing, that I should shake it off and forget about it."

"Absolutely," Mom says.

"You're a big part of the team," Dad adds. "They need you."

"Of course they need her," Grandma Gold shouts. "Although I would have liked to see you skate in something new after driving forever in the pouring rain."

I stare at Becca. My mouth is hanging open. I can't believe it. She's lying. Unless the coach said those things before I got there . . . but from the look on Ruthless's face, and what I heard, it certainly didn't seem like it.

Grandma Gold leans over to slap Alex's back. "And how's our high school basketball star?"

Alex peels off his headphones and says, "Huh?"

"Still the top scorer on the team?" she asks.

"Yeah," he says. "When are we going to order?"

"They're so busy," Mom says, waving to a Synchronettes mom across the restaurant. "I'm sure our waiter will come soon."

"And what about you, Calli? What are you up to these days?" Grandma Gold asks, peering at me. I swear, it's just like she knows the ABC game, except she did it out of order.

Before I can answer, Dad says happily, "Calli is going to be an actress!"

"Oh." Grandma Gold nods. "Like Marjorie?"

Dad folds his arms across his chest. "Yeah, except Calli won't end up like her."

Grandma Gold pours three packets of Sweet'n Low into her coffee. "Who knows what went through that girl's head?" she says. "Got herself a big part in a play, had an agent and everything, then went and threw it all away." The spoon clinks against the side of the cup as she stirs.

Dad looks at me. "What are you going to have, Calli?"

89

"Pancakes," I reply.

"Me too," he says with a thumbs-up. Dad and I both love pancakes for dinner.

"Oh, that reminds me," Grandma Gold interrupts. "Have you talked to Joel lately?"

"Mother." Dad looks uncomfortable. "You know Joel and I don't really talk."

"Since when?" She sets her cup back on the saucer and some coffee sloshes over the side.

"Since . . . the last few years."

"Well," Grandma Gold says, "*if* you were talking to your brother, you would have known that he was written up in some big magazine. I can't remember the name . . . Snazzy . . . Jazzy . . . ? Anyway, he's listed as the top plastic surgeon in all of California."

"Is that so?" Dad says. "Terrific."

"You bet it's terrific. My Joel really made something of himself."

"Oh, here's the waiter," Mom interrupts. "Let's order." She puts her hand on Dad's arm and they glance at each other.

I ask for chocolate chip pancakes and hot chocolate, but when the waiter brings the cup, it's not steaming and there's no whipped cream. Grandma and Dad and Mom go back to talking about Becca and Alex, and me starting out in theater, and how we're all the greatest kids in the entire world.

"I'll be in the front row for all of your productions."
Grandma Gold winks at me.

I stare up at the chandelier in the entryway and notice
a couple of burned-out bulbs. I wonder how Pete and the
workers here find the time to change them. The restaurant is always so busy.

Our food comes, and Becca's friend Taylor stops by
our table with her mom. Grandma Gold asks me, "You
think you'll do *Beauty and the Beast*? I love that one."

Mom asks Taylor's mom for her opinion on the
skaters' hairpieces, and Dad starts mapping out a defensive plan with Alex for next week's basketball game. The
table gets noisy, and I'm trying to cut my pancakes and
sip my lukewarm hot chocolate and listen to all the
conversations. But after a while, I can't tell any of their
voices apart.

Noodle Colors

$\mathcal{I}$t's PHP time again. Noah and I are supposed to be creating a mosaic face out of different colors of dry pasta, but we're sitting at his desk with a heap of noodles, a bottle of glue, and an empty piece of construction paper.

At least Noah's sitting on a chair and isn't under the desk.

"I told you," he says. "I can't make stuff."

"Do you want to try?"

"No."

"Everyone else is making one," I point out.

"So?"

I look over at Claire, a few desks away. Her mosaic noodle face looks like it could be in a museum. She and her peer are concentrating on the placement of every single piece.

I look back at Noah, who is separating the noodles into piles by color.

"This is a dumb project," he scoffs. "How can you make noodles look like a face, anyway?"

I giggle. "I agree," I whisper. "It is kind of dumb."

He glances at me; then the two of us sit in silence, Noah shifting around the noodles and me watching the other PHP teams busy at work. The whole room is quiet, and Mrs. Lamont and Mrs. Bezner are walking from desk to desk, admiring the creations. I hope they don't come over here.

I promised myself I wouldn't give up on Noah, but he's not making it easy. I'm about to suggest that we try to make something—it doesn't have to be a face—when Noah points toward Tanya Timley and says, "She's a red."

"What?" I ask.

"Like a fire engine."

I tip my head. "Huh? You mean she has red hair?"

"No," Noah replies, then points at Wanda. "She's a blue," he says. "A blue sky. With no clouds."

I look at Noah, then at Wanda and Tanya.

"Don't you know people are colors?" he asks.

"I guess I didn't."

"You can't see it?"

"Is it bad if I say no?"

He shakes his head. "Sometimes you have to look really hard."

"Oh," I say, and concentrate as hard as I can on the back of Claire's head. After a few minutes, though, I admit, "I can't see a color."

"It's okay," he says. "Most people can't do it."

"How can you?"

"I just can," he says, squinting down at his piles of noodles.

I open the bottle of glue, pour some onto the construction paper, and aimlessly tack down some noodles.

"Are you making a face?" Noah asks.

I shrug and reach for more noodles. Noah hands me a few and we glue them down together.

"I still think this is dumb," he says, and I nod.

"So, what color are you?" I ask. I guess that he'll answer black, or white, or no color at all.

He replies, "A whole bunch of mixed-up colors."

"Oh. . . . Were you ever just one?" I ask.

"I can't remember."

I close the bottle of glue. "And me?"

He places a noodle on the paper very carefully and, without looking in my direction, says, "Pink."

"Pink. Is that good?"

"Pink," he repeats. "Heart," he adds. "Pink heart."

I get the same feeling inside as when I made Noah laugh—all warm and mushy—like my chest is going to burst open. I've never felt that way in a class or a sport or an activity.

I think that's good.

Will I get that feeling in improv? It would certainly make Dad's heart burst if I did.

I smile at Noah but he doesn't see. He's putting every single last noodle on the paper like he's in a noodle marathon.

"Doesn't look like a face," he says when he's finished.

"But we made something." I hold up the paper carefully so none of the noodles will move.

He stares at me, then at the paper. "But it's not anything."

"It is. There are colors."

He examines the paper again. Then it's time for the fifth graders to leave.

"I'll see you next time," I say, and as I'm walking away, Noah gives me a tiny, small, but possibly happy wave. And I wave back.

Definite progress.

The next day, after school, I'm not upset that I have to go to the skating rink with Becca and Mom, because I'm hoping that Noah will be there, maybe even sitting at a table in the concession area. But when we get there, I don't see him anywhere.

The rink is back to normal after the exhibition, except

for about twenty huge black garbage bags stacked by the back door. I see the dad on his laptop computer, the kid with the DEATH RULES hoodie lurking around the arcade, and the twins, but no Noah.

Becca is acting like nothing is wrong. I'm sure she has decided to step it up and rise to the challenge, like Dad would advise her to. She seems to be skating fine. While I'm watching, she doesn't make any mistakes.

After we're there just a few minutes, Mom waves a yellow Post-it at me and says, "I'm going to run you over to the dentist. Luckily, I don't have a meeting. We'll come back to get Becca."

All the assistants at Dr. Cannon's office, and even Dr. Cannon, the dentist, talk to kids like they're two years old. They make you put this purple stuff on your teeth to show where you're not brushing well, and they call the saliva sucker Mr. Thirsty. If that's not bad enough, they ask if you want to pick a prize from the treasure chest when you're done.

While we're there, Mom spends the whole time on her phone and I can hear her voice even though I'm down the hall from the waiting room. She's talking about the hairpiece issue and why the new costumes haven't arrived. Then she calls Dad to confirm what time Alex's game is.

The assistant tells me I have beautiful teeth but if I don't take care of them better, they might not stay so beautiful. I get a picture in my mind of Tanya Timley's shiny white teeth, and when the assistant turns her back,

I make a face at her. I know she didn't see, because she still gives me a sticker with big smiling teeth that says GREAT CHECKUP!

On our way out, I take a little notepad from the treasure chest. There's a photo of a polar bear on the cover.

We rush back to the rink to get Becca, then drop her off and rush to Alex's game. Afterward, he stays late for a team meeting. On the way home, Mom glances at me in the backseat of the van. "Tomorrow you won't have to do all this running around with me," she says. "You have your first improv class! Are you excited? Nervous?"

"Yeah," I mumble. What color would Noah see for Mom? Electric orange?

"What if I don't like the class?" I ask.

"Now, you don't want to start out with a bad attitude."

"But what if I don't?"

"Calli Gold, I don't want to hear that. We discussed this, remember?"

Even though I told myself I would try improv and be a Gold like the rest of them, deep down inside, I really don't want to. A strange feeling rears up. "You're not going to talk about the piano again, are you?" My voice comes out mean. Like Becca's.

"No . . . ," she says.

I can't stop myself. "You know, Mom, if you're so sad about never getting to play the piano when you were a kid, you could still learn. Why don't you take lessons now? Then you could stop being sorry you never got to."

I can see part of her face and it looks crumpled and hurt. I bite my lip. In the space above her head, I imagine a big black piano with sharp white claws instead of keys. The claw piano looks like it's going to pounce on her. Or me.

Without another word, she pulls into the garage, gets out of the van, and leaves me inside, which makes me feel worse than if she had yelled.

I feel like all the pink has drained out of me.

CLIC

The next day, as if nothing happened, Mom is driving me to the first improv class. I know she's mad at me, but whenever I try to tell her I'm sorry, the words just won't come out.

She pulls the van up to the front walkway of the community center but doesn't turn off the engine. She peels my yellow Post-it off the steering wheel. "The class is in room seven," she says flatly.

"You're not coming in with me?" I ask, a little shaky.

"Do I need to?" she says, turning to look at me. "I thought you told me you want to do more things on your own, and stay home by yourself, like Wanda does."

"Yeah, but I don't know anyone in the class."

"Oh, I wouldn't worry. I'm sure you'll make a new friend."

I slowly reach for the door handle.

"You'll be fine," she says. "I'll be waiting out front in an hour when the class is over."

She starts pulling away from the curb before the van door is completely closed. The air is cold against my cheeks and it's starting to get dark. I can think of only one choice. To go inside.

When I get to room seven, I stop outside the door and stand on the flat gray carpet. My feet don't want to move any farther than the doorway.

"Are you here for improv?" a voice calls out, and I look up to see a woman in a black turtleneck waving at me from inside the room. Perched on a metal chair, she's wearing a pair of black-rimmed trendy-type glasses, the kind people wear even if they don't need them.

When I nod, she gestures to me. "Come on down, then."

I trudge inside and see five kids sitting in metal chairs across from the woman. A tall, skinny man is next to her, also wearing a black turtleneck. They look just like the people on the brochure, even though they're not the same ones. Maybe it's a rule that everyone who works in improv has to wear a black turtleneck. Would Noah be able to see any other color for them except black?

When I take a seat, the kid next to me turns. It's the creepy kid from the skating rink, the one with the DEATH RULES hoodie. I can't believe it. He does improv?

"We might as well get started." The woman stands

up. "Welcome to Improv 101. I'm Liza. And this"—she sweeps her arm toward the man—"is Gary. We are going to acquaint you with the amazing world of improvisational theater over the next four weeks." Both of them stand up and take a bow, and a girl behind me claps, but no one else does.

"All right, then. Everyone stand up!" Liza orders.

Reluctantly, we rise. I wonder if anyone really wants to be here.

"We're going to start out by teaching you the four major principles of improv." Liza pulls off her fake glasses and waves them wildly. "Gary?"

Gary leaps from his chair, stamps one foot, and shouts, "Click!"

No one except the girl who clapped says anything. She repeats, "Click?" and writes something in a small spiral.

Liza strides over to a dry-erase board and scrawls four huge letters: *C, L, I, C.*

"Click!" Gary shouts again.

The kid with the hoodie looks at me but I quickly look away.

"Clarity," Liza says.

"Listening," Gary says.

"Instinct." Liza again.

Then they shout together: "Confidence."

The girl with the spiral gasps, "Oh, I get it, CLIC!"

"Ten points for you," Gary singsongs, clapping with only the tips of his fingers.

Liza writes the four words on the dry-erase board. "When you do improv," she explains, "you need to be free to express yourself and your vision. That's *clarity*. Always *listen* to your fellow actors, use your *instincts*, and most of all, have *confidence* in yourself."

I know, right then and there, in room seven of the Southbrook Community Center, that improv is not going to be my passion. All I can think about is how hot my feet are inside my shoes, how I won't be able to get through the rest of these classes, and how I'll never find something I'm good at in this world. I definitely don't have the feeling I had when Noah said I was a pink heart. On top of all that, I don't have a clue what Liza is talking about.

Gary asks us to get into a circle. "We're going to play a little warm-up game." He pushes away the chairs. "We're all going to say our names. But here's the catch: no one can say their names at the same time. If you do, you're out. Keep saying your name, watch your fellow actors closely, and let's see what happens."

He shouts, "Gary," and the girl with the spiral calls out, "Megan." A boy says, "Andrew," and another girl blurts, "Lauren." Liza shouts her name and Gary calls his again.

There is silence; then the hoodie kid and I say our names at the same time.

"You're both out," Gary cries. "Too bad. Have a seat."

I sink into my chair and cross my arms in front of my chest. The hoodie kid starts biting the skin on his thumb.

Gary and Liza are the last two people left standing, which is of course not fair at all.

Liza pushes her glasses to the top of her head and gazes intently at us. "Wasn't that amazing? Did you feel it? And that's just the tip of the iceberg!"

Next she asks everyone to find a partner, which is a completely bad thing when you don't know anyone in the class. The hoodie kid glances at me, and I grumble, "Fine."

Gary explains that this will be our first real improvisational exercise. He tells us that one person will say a word and the other person will say another, and we have to keep going back and forth to create a skit. This doesn't sound too bad, because no one can get "out," but then Gary mentions that we'll be doing it in front of everyone else. My palms get all sweaty.

"We'll demonstrate," Gary says, and he and Liza start bouncing words off each other like Ping-Pong balls. In about thirty seconds, they have some funny skit going about zebras that escaped from the zoo and are running around eating petunias. Pretty much everyone is cracking up except me.

Liza and Gary stop and take a quick bow; then Gary points to the hoodie kid and me. "You're up."

The two of us stand and the hoodie kid says in a low, menacing voice, "Evil."

I frown and glance at Gary.

"Just say the first word that pops into your mind," he says.

I glance at the kid's sweatshirt. "Rules," I call out.

"In," the hoodie kid replies.

"The."

"Land."

"Of."

"Grujorken!" the hoodie kid shouts.

I know I look completely confused.

We end up with something about evil people in a magical land who have frequent nosebleeds. No one is laughing.

Everyone else takes a turn; then Liza informs us that class is over for today. "Your homework," she says, "is to come up with an occupation, a place, and a food that you will give to someone else next week to incorporate into a skit."

"What's an occupation again?" It's the girl with the spiral. I am beginning to dislike her.

"A job," Gary drawls. "Waiter, garbage man, funeral director. Use your imagination."

I think he's going to talk about bringing out the inner muse, but he doesn't.

"Good work today, people," Liza says as we put our jackets on. "See you all next week!" She waves her glasses at us.

When I push open the doors of the community

center, Mom's waiting in the van. Big puffs of steam are coming from the back end.

"How was it?" she asks when I get in.

"Okay."

"Tell me about it. What did you do?"

"Dumb stuff." I sound like Noah.

"You didn't like it?"

I look out the window. It's foggy and dirty and cold. I drag one finger across the glass and scrawl a big heart.

"Not really."

The rest of the drive home, we are both quiet.

View from the Top of the Hill

*a*s the days go on, I rush between home and the rink and Alex's games and back home again. I struggle my way through one more improv class, but the second one is even worse than the first. The hoodie kid now thinks we're friends, and the girl with the spiral kept answering every question Gary and Liza asked. They love her.

Dad bought me a bunch of books on the craft of acting. He told me I'll move on soon enough from the class at the community center and he's researching the best acting studios in the area.

I complained to Wanda and Claire about the improv class and Wanda said, "Tell your parents that you hate it and want to quit."

"You don't get it," I said. "My parents are desperate. They need me to find something I'm successful at. That's what people do in my family."

"Just tell them you hate it," Wanda repeated, as if it was the easiest thing in the world.

I haven't seen Noah in a while and I sort of miss him, in a strange way. We had to skip a PHP time, because his class went on a field trip. I hope Noah had someone to sit with on the bus ride and that he didn't have to make a project afterward. I wonder if he's made any friends in his class.

It's almost December. Every day at school, Wanda gives me the weather report. Since the three of us met in kindergarten, we've gone sledding together when it snows for the first time.

This year Claire said she thought we were getting too old for our tradition. Wanda was furious.

"We are not," Wanda insisted. "You agree with me, right, Calli?"

I remembered all the times the three of us whizzed down the hill by the junior high, screaming and laughing. "I don't think we're too old," I said. Then I think Claire felt like we were two against one and she had to agree.

Becca has been extra snippy to me, which makes me wonder if she did see me watching when Coach Ruthless was criticizing her at the exhibition. She's not the kind of sister to sit down and have a heart-to-heart talk, but if she was, I'd tell her that I won't breathe a word to Mom or Dad. But she doesn't give me a chance to be the kind of sister I want to be.

On a cloudy, chilly Friday, Wanda practically knocks me over when I walk into school. "Six inches!" she says. "Tomorrow!"

"Really?"

"An unusually early snow. Lucky for us, huh? Get your sled ready!"

In the classroom, Mrs. Lamont asks everyone to settle down. Wanda's definitely having trouble with that.

"Boys and girls," Mrs. Lamont says, "before we get started on our work today, I want to tell you how pleased Mrs. Bezner and I are with the Peer Helper Program." She clasps her hands together. "The program is turning out better than we ever could have imagined. And all of you are responsible for its success."

She smooths her long skirt and continues. "Now, you all know we're getting close to the holiday season. Usually, we collect for the needy, or have a holiday party, but this year, Mrs. Bezner and I came up with something even better. We will be putting together a PHP Friendship Fair."

A few of the kids start to ask questions, but Mrs. Lamont puts up her hands to tell us to be quiet. "What better way to celebrate the success of our PHP and the joy of the season than with a fair? Each of you, along with your peer, will design a booth demonstrating what friendship means to you. You'll have about three weeks to work on these—we'll add in some extra meeting time—then, just before winter break, we will invite our families to the fair and show off all of your wonderful projects. And I know they will be wonderful."

Several kids raise their hands now. All I can think is, how can Noah and I possibly put together a booth for a big fair? We could barely glue noodles on construction paper.

Tanya Timley juts her hand into the air. "Question," she sings. "Would it be possible to use an electrical outlet?"

"I think that can be arranged," Mrs. Lamont says.

"Yay," Tanya cheers. "I won't reveal my idea, but if Ashley and I are on the same page, which we usually are, we might need to plug something in."

I stick my tongue out at Tanya behind her back. She already has an idea? I make a secret wish that the toothpaste people don't like Tanya Timley one bit and reject her.

My walk home that day is filled with worry about what Noah and I can come up with for the fair, but I feel better the next morning when I wake up and see that Wanda was right. Snow covers everything in sight— wonderful, pure white snow. The street, trees, and grass are glinting like a million jewels in the sun, and I feel like the snow has fallen just for me.

Claire's mom drops off Wanda and Claire at my house right after breakfast. Wanda is stamping her boots in the snow, making a design of tread marks on our drive-way. "I love this," she calls as I join them outside.

"My dad has to get my sled." I point to a purple plastic sled on a high shelf in the garage.

"Tell him to hurry!" Wanda urges.

Claire glances at Wanda. "Calm down," she says. "It's only snow."

"Only snow?" Wanda dances around. "It's the first snow!"

Mom pokes her head out. "Hi, girls," she says. "I thought I heard voices." She claps a hand to her cheek. "Claire, you must have grown three inches since I last saw you!" Claire beams.

"Mom," I interrupt. "Can you ask Dad to get my sled?"

"Sure."

"Mother!" Becca wails from inside the house, and Mom smiles. "Excuse me," she says. "I'll send Dad out."

"Probably stubbed her toe," Wanda says when Mom closes the door, and I giggle.

Dad comes out, zipping his jacket. "Which one?" he asks, and I point to the high shelf. He pretends to protest. "All the way up there?"

"It's the best sled."

"Well, okay, then."

Dad stands on a ladder to reach the sled, then hands it to me. "I'll drive you girls over to the hill," he offers. "We'll take Mom's van. More room."

We pile our sleds, saucers, and snowboards in the trunk. Dad gestures to me. "Why don't you get in front, Calli?"

I shake my head. "Mom doesn't let me sit in front yet. I think I don't weigh quite enough."

He leans down and winks. "Aw, you're close enough, aren't you? It's just a few minutes' ride." He puts a finger to his lips. "It'll be our secret."

I settle myself importantly in the front seat next to Dad, and Wanda and Claire get in back. I'm sure that Alex and Becca didn't get to sit in front when they were my age. Becca would probably complain that I'm getting special privileges because I'm the baby of the family, but I don't care. I can see all the dials and knobs, and I could even control the radio if I wanted to.

"How's school, everyone?" Dad asks cheerfully as he backs out of the driveway.

"Fine," we say in unison.

"Great thing that kids today still go sledding. Get away from all those electronics once in a while," he says.

"Yeah," we reply.

"I remember the first time we took Calli sledding." He chuckles. "She couldn't have been more than three or four at the time."

Oh, no, I think, and glance back at Wanda and Claire.

"We packed her in the sled, pushed her off, and halfway down the hill, she toppled out the side and fell headfirst into the snow." Dad lets out a laugh. "I think she cried for two days afterwards."

"There's the junior high. The hill's right over there," I interrupt, and point, wishing Dad would stop the embarrassing story.

At the hill, we get our stuff; then he waves to us as he drives away. I watch the puff of steam from the back of the van disappear in the cold air. "Sorry," I sigh, shaking my head.

"Don't worry," Wanda says. "Dads are like that. They live to embarrass us."

"At least yours are around," Claire says, then looks over at the sledding hill. "I still think we're getting too old for this."

Wanda grabs Claire's arm. "See those guys over there?" she says, gesturing to a group that beat us to the hill. "I happen to know they're in eighth grade! They're not too old for sledding!"

"What else were you going to do today, anyway?" I ask Claire.

She looks at the hill, then back at us. Finally, she grins. "Okay, okay. You've convinced me."

Wanda grabs my gloved hand and Claire's as well. "We always go together the first time down the hill. It can't be any other way."

The three of us pile into the longest sled—Wanda in front, me in the middle, and Claire in the back. We're pretty squeezed in now that we've all gotten taller and bigger, but it doesn't matter. We dig our hands into the snow to push off, and then sail downward, making a clean first path on our part of the hill.

Claire screams in my ear—she always does—and Wanda lets go of the sides and sticks her arms high into the air. The wind is sharp and cold against my cheeks. We coast to a stop and the three of us tumble out. When we finally stand up, the snow reaches the tops of our boots.

"Let's climb back up!" Wanda yells, and we stomp up the hill. Wanda grabs a saucer, plops down on her stomach, pushes off, and flies down. I follow her on a smaller sled, and we wave to Claire, who's still at the top, and yell, "Come on!" Claire positions herself neatly on a snowboard and floats down the hill toward us without falling.

"Show-off!" Wanda calls, and when Claire reaches us, Wanda pops up and pushes her over. We laugh and run up the hill again, dragging the sled and saucer and snowboard behind us.

All my worries disappear in the crisp, cool whiteness of the snow and the open clear blue of the sky.

After we've gone down the hill about fifty times, we drop to the ground. The air is warmer now and the snow is getting slushier. Wanda picks up a gloveful of snow and licks it.

"Ew." Claire frowns. "You know that's probably polluted. Loaded with chemicals."

"So what? It tastes good." Wanda takes a bite of snow and smiles at us.

Wanda's and Claire's cheeks have cheerful red patches on them, which means mine do too. That's what I love about winter—the way the cool air makes my skin tingle and come alive.

I look across the long, open field at the bottom of the hill. The redbrick junior high building stands across the street, empty and silent and big. "We'll be there next year," I say, pointing.

"Done with elementary school at last," Wanda replies happily. "Actually, I'm ready for sixth grade right now."

"I'm not sure if I'm ready," I admit.

"My cousin turned into a completely different person in junior high," Claire says. "Dyed her hair and pierced her eyebrow and started wearing all black."

"That won't happen to us," Wanda says. "My mom won't let me even get my ears pierced."

I shade my eyes with a wet glove. "We'll still be friends, won't we?"

"Of course," Wanda shouts.

"People change," Claire says.

"But not us." Wanda takes another bite of snow.

"Hey!" I say. "Let's make a pact. Let's make a pact to stay friends even if we change in junior high like Claire's cousin and pierce something. What do you say?"

I take hold of each of their gloves; then we stack our

hands vertically. I solemnly state each of our first initials. "W, C, C." I stare at them. "Hey, that's WC squared."

"WC squared," Wanda repeats. "Friends no matter what happens in junior high."

We hold our hands together in silence; then Claire pulls hers out. Wanda and I take ours away too. Wanda says, "My butt is freezing."

"Mine too." I laugh.

"Do my braces have icicles on them?" Wanda grins, baring her top metal row.

I shake my head and grin back at her.

"Why does snow have to be so cold?" Claire stands and brushes off the back of her jacket.

I clutch both of their sleeves. "Let's go down the hill one more time. Together."

We pile into the biggest sled and the three of us skate down the hill. One last time on the first snow of fifth grade. WC Squared.

The Calendar Crisis

Mrs. Lamont posts a sheet with all the extra dates we will be meeting with our peers. The Friendship Fair will be held the week before winter break starts, Thursday night at seven o'clock in the gym.

"Perfect!" Tanya exclaims. Her desk is still next to mine, unfortunately. We won't change desks until after break. "I'm leaving that Friday for Mexico," she says. I'm not sure if she's talking to me or just to the general air around her. "I'm filming a commercial, so my family gets a free trip. How cool is that?"

I wonder if she expects me to answer. I look at her teeth. Maybe she got the toothpaste commercial after all. Tanya glances over at me, as if daring me to say that I have something better planned over break, which, of course, I do not.

Tanya jiggles her hand in the air. "Mrs. Lamont! Don't forget that Ashley and I need to plug something in for our display. Of course, I need to talk to her, but I'm pretty sure I know what we'll be doing."

"I didn't forget, Tanya." Mrs. Lamont still has her shoes on, since it's the morning, but even so, I can see that today her socks have little green and red frogs on them.

Mrs. Lamont picks up a stack of papers and asks Wanda and me to hand them out to the class. "Be sure to give your families these flyers about the date and time of the Friendship Fair," she says.

"The fair is going to be so much fun," Wanda whispers as we start passing out the flyers.

"Yeah." I wonder if Noah and I are going to have anything to show. We're supposed to come up with ideas this week.

Tanya takes a flyer and actually says thank you. She scans it, then raises her hand again. "Mrs. Lamont," she says, frowning, "I don't see a diagram of the booths."

"Mrs. Bezner and I will randomly assign booths that night when the gym is set up," Mrs. Lamont says.

"Randomly assign?" Tanya repeats, as if she's never heard of that concept.

"Well, yes."

"If it's all right, I'd like to request a certain space in the gym."

Mrs. Lamont raises her eyebrows like she is trying not

117

to look annoyed. "Write me a note, Tanya," she says. "And I'll see what I can do."

Wanda rolls her eyes. "Do you think her hair is really that color, or she dyes it?" she whispers to me.

I shrug and continue down the row of desks with the flyers.

Wanda narrows her eyes. "I bet it's dyed."

When I get home, the first thing I do is take a yellow Post-it and write *Friendship Fair 7 p.m.* Then I pull a stool from the counter over to the Calendar. I climb up and find the right Thursday.

I see a pink Post-it and a blue one already on that day. Becca's says *skating competition, time TBA,* and Alex's says *home game, 5:30 p.m.*

I'm standing there atop the stool, holding my measly yellow Post-it, when I hear Mom's voice behind me. "Calli! Be careful! What are you doing?"

"I have something to put on the Calendar." I turn, waving the Post-it. Then something awful happens. My foot slips. The stool shakes. Then it topples out from under me and I go flying through the air. As I'm falling, I desperately clutch at something. The Calendar. I hit the kitchen floor with a big corner piece of it in one hand and my little yellow Post-it in the other.

Mom lets out a scream. "Are you okay?"

I stand up sheepishly and rub my side. "I'm fine."

She looks me over. "You sure you're not hurt? Can you walk? Do you feel dizzy?" She puts a hand on my forehead.

"Mom, I'm fine."

She sets the stool upright, then slowly gazes up at the Calendar.

"I'm sorry," I say with a gulp.

"It wasn't your fault," she whispers. She reaches for the corner I've torn from the Calendar, then opens a drawer and takes out a roll of tape. She fits the ripped section back into place, then secures it with several long pieces of tape. A few Post-its fluttered to the floor when I fell. She picks those up and firmly places them back on the correct dates.

"I don't think I could live without this calendar," she says with a nervous chuckle. "What were you doing up there, anyway?"

"Here," I say, handing her my Post-it. "This goes on the Thursday before winter break."

"What is it?" Mom looks at the note.

I reach inside my backpack and pull out the flyer. "This explains everything. It's a big thing at school. We're doing this Friendship Fair with our second-grade peers. Part of the Peer Helper Program. Remember I told you about it?"

"Oh," she says, and takes the flyer from me, reads it, then holds my Post-it up to the Calendar. She sticks it just below Becca's and Alex's, then turns to me. "Honestly, Calli, I don't know how we're going to squeeze this in."

I stare at her, unable to speak. My heart starts to pound.

"Becca has her first competition, and the Lady Reds will be there. And this is a crucial game for Alex," she says. "Those things were already on the Calendar."

I cross my arms. "So?"

"Well, let me think." She rubs her forehead. "We certainly can't be in three places at once . . . and I don't even know the exact time of the competition at this point. I guess Dad and I can split up, and one of us can bring you to the fair when either the game or the competition ends."

Something inside me boils up, and my skin gets hot and prickly. My voice rushes out like I'm not in control of it. "I can't be late. And are you saying either you or Dad wouldn't come? All the other families will be there. This is something important! To me! Don't you understand?"

I grab my backpack and stomp upstairs, then slam the door to my room. I start kicking and throwing pillows and stuffed animals off my bed; then I thrash around and mess up my comforter. Even though my lip is quivering and my eyes feel watery, I promise myself I won't cry.

Finally, when I feel tired out, I hang upside down from the bed with my head nearly touching the carpet. I dig deep inside me and find the courage to whisper the truth. "Sometimes I really hate this family."

No one calls me for dinner. Maybe they forgot about me. Maybe Mom cautioned everyone to let me cool off. She's big on that when someone has a fit. At six-thirty, I decide to go downstairs. Everyone is in their usual seats and Mom is putting a plate of chicken on the table. Before I sit down, I glance at the taped-up Calendar and I'm happy to see that my yellow Post-it has not been removed. Yet.

Dad has already started the ABC game and Alex is telling him something about a new basketball play. Mom slides a piece of chicken onto my dish as Dad moves on to Becca.

"My L.A. teacher said only one student got a hundred on the pronoun quiz, and that one student was me," Becca declares proudly.

"Way to go." Dad nods, then turns to me.

I have that boiling, prickly feeling again.

"Number three?" He raises his eyebrows. "Your turn."

That does it.

I take a deep breath. "I have an actual, real, important activity that I put on the Calendar today, but it seems that this family is too busy to care about me or anything that I might want to do."

The four of them stare at me.

Becca glances toward the wall and says, "What happened to the Calendar?"

"Why is Becca's and Alex's stuff more important than my fair?" I cry.

No one says anything.

"All this family cares about is what everyone can do, not how people feel." I stand up and march out of the kitchen. Even though I'm really hungry, I decide not to eat so they will feel even more awful.

As I'm going upstairs, I hear Becca mutter, "What's up with her?"

A few minutes later, after I've cried about a thousand tears (I couldn't hold them back this time), there's a light knock on my bedroom door. Mom walks in and sits down next to me on the bed.

"Calli," she starts.

"Don't talk to me," I yell. "I don't want to hear your reasons why I have to be late and you can't come." I stuff my face in a mushy pillow.

She pats me on the back. "All I came up to tell you is that we'll find a way to work it out," she says, smoothing my hair. "You know, these are good problems to have. It's good to be busy. That's what life's all about."

No, I think, that's not what life is all about. "I'm going to the fair. I'm not going to be late either. We have to be there an hour before to set up."

Mom stares at me.

"I'm not going with one of you to the game or the competition," I say. "I'm going to the fair. I don't care if any of you come or not, but I'm going."

An Idea

Now not only is Becca acting cool around me, Mom is too. I don't know what's happening to me. It's like quiet Calli is being taken over by a mad, emotional Calli who keeps having outbursts. And every day when I walk into the kitchen, the rip in the Calendar is a reminder of my tantrums. The worst part is that there's no one to talk to about all this. Not Becca, never Becca. Alex is busy with basketball, and as close as I am with Wanda and Claire, they don't really understand what life is like in my family. It would be nice to have someone who would get it without my having to explain.

At school, Mrs. Lamont tells us that we're having a shortened gym period so we can get together with our peers and plan the Friendship Fair. I'm happy because I'll get to see Noah, and gym is not my favorite subject. We still have to change into our gym shoes, though.

This turns out to be a waste, because all we do is sit and listen. Ms. Pector informs us that after winter break, we will be starting the health unit. Today is a little overview.

"Puberty," Ms. Pector begins, and the boys immediately erupt into fits of laughter. "Quiet!" she commands. "Puberty is a time of wonder," she continues. "We will be learning about the remarkable changes that will be happening to each and every one of you."

From the corner of my eye, I catch Wanda sneaking a peek at her chest. Claire pokes her in the back. Tanya Timley is sitting up straight and tall in front of me, and when I look at the back of her shirt, this time I do see the outline of a bra.

I point it out to Wanda, who gasps. Claire jabs both of us.

Ms. Pector is saying these embarrassing, private words with no shame, and all the boys are laughing again, plus snorting and slapping their legs. Jason starts chanting the word "uterus" over and over, making it sound like he's cheering for the uterus team. Pretty soon all the boys are chanting it along with him. "U-ter-us! U-ter-us!"

Ms. Pector blows her whistle loudly and the boys stop. "Might I remind you," she says, "that you will be tested on all of this information, so it *is* to be taken seriously."

With the boys still whispering, "U-ter-us," we walk to Mrs. Bezner's room, and when we get inside, I see that Noah's chair is empty. I find him under his desk.

I duck underneath and I'm about to ask him why he's there, but he pulls a deck of cards from his pocket—the most tattered, worn deck of cards I've ever seen.

"Want to see a trick?" he asks.

"Sure."

I know we're supposed to be talking about the fair, but I watch as Noah fans out the deck. "Pick a card."

I pull one out; then he closes up the deck, has me stick my card in the middle, and shuffles. Noah starts laying out cards on the floor. "Is this your card?" He points to the seven of spades.

"No," I say.

He nods. "This one?" The three of hearts.

I shake my head.

"Right," he says, "because it's this one." He holds up the two of diamonds.

"That's it," I reply. "How did you do that?"

"I can't tell you." He gathers up the cards and stuffs the deck back into his pocket.

"That was amazing, Noah!"

The two of us sit there for a while. I can hear the others planning away.

"So," I say, "do you have any ideas of what we can do for the Friendship Fair?"

He makes a face at me.

"Let me guess," I say. "You're not good at thinking of ideas."

He nods, but I think I see a little smile too.

"Is that why you're back under here?" I ask softly.

"Maybe." He looks down at the carpet.

"Let's try to think of something together. We have to think of *something*, or else you and I are going to have an empty table the night of the fair."

"Why do we have to?" Noah asks.

"Well, everyone else is, and besides, maybe it will be fun. Did you ever think about that?"

He doesn't say anything. A feeling of panic creeps into my stomach. After I made that big scene with my family, now I'm not going to have a booth even if a miracle happens and they do manage to come. "Everyone is thinking of ideas," I say, peeking out from under the desk.

Noah pulls up his knees and buries his face between them. "You should work with someone else."

I think about how he said I was a pink heart. "I don't want to work with someone else."

"Why not?" His voice is very small, like him.

"I don't know. . . I just want to work with you."

"But why?"

I can't help laughing. "Why do you ask so many questions?"

Now Noah's voice is soft and scared-sounding. "Because no one ever answers them," he says.

I look at him, all tucked into his body. I gently touch his arm. "You don't have to hide from me."

He jerks his head up and looks like he might cry. "People don't tell you stuff when you're a kid. They keep all kinds of grown-up secrets."

"Like what?"

"Like about what's wrong with you."

I wait as Noah twists his hands. "One doctor says one thing and another doctor says another thing, and I don't know what any of them are talking about. Mom says between me and my sister and her job, she's going to have a nervous breakdown."

"Your mom works a lot?" I ask.

"Yeah," he says, then frowns. "They keep telling the doctors they just want me to be normal. Like everybody else."

"Your mom and dad?"

"Yeah."

I nod. "Parents are like that," I say, thinking of Dad, and how he wants me to be a Gold like the rest of my family.

"They said I might have some kind of syndrome. But they don't know yet. They give me tests and ask a lot of questions." He glances at me. "What's a syndrome?"

"I don't know. Like a disease?"

"I guess." He shrugs. "The doctors all said one thing. That it's hard to diag— What's that word again?"

"Diagnose?"

"Yeah. That." Noah looks at me. "Don't tell anyone," he adds nervously. "It's a secret."

"I won't."

Noah and I sit quietly under the desk for a few more minutes; then he adds, "You promise?"

"I do. I promise. It's our secret." Then I stare wide-eyed at Noah.

"What?" he asks.

"That's it," I say. "Noah! Friends keep each other's secrets. That can be our theme for the Friendship Fair!"

He gives me a confused look. "I don't get it."

"Well, the best kind of friends tell their secrets to each other but they keep them, right? A good friend would never tell, like how I just now promised you that I would keep your secret."

He nods slowly.

"So can we make a project or something about that?" I ask.

Noah's face looks crumpled and worried.

"I know. You told me. You can't make stuff." I bob my head. "But we'll come up with something that doesn't require doing a lot of art. Whaddya think?"

He doesn't answer, then says very softly, "Are you my friend?"

My heart is flying. "Yes," I say without taking a breath. "I am."

He pushes his glasses up on his nose. "Really?"

"Yes."

He gives me that little half smile. "I think we have an idea."

"We do," I say, and I can't help it; I reach a hand out and smooth down his messy hair. It perks right back up again, and I laugh.

On the way out, I hear Wanda and Claire enthusiastically describing their booths to each other. Wanda needs Play-Doh and Claire is worrying about how she and her peer will have enough time to create their complicated exhibit. Tanya says her booth is going to "blow everyone else's away."

I don't care. Not one bit.

Noah and I have an idea.

Stones

The next time I'm going to the rink, I cross my fingers and hope that Noah will be there so we can talk about our idea. Most of the groups are way ahead of us. Becca spends the entire van ride telling Mom about a girl on her team who takes every opportunity she can to toss a mean comment at her. I wonder if it was the girl who Becca almost tripped at the exhibition.

"Can't you do something?" Becca twirls a piece of hair with a finger.

"I think you're going to have to work this one out yourself," Mom says. Becca huffs but I want to applaud.

I'm thrilled to find Noah inside the rink, even if he is under the hockey-foosball table. I see the hoodie kid heading my way—he probably wants to bond over the improv experience—but I kneel down by Noah and say, "Hey."

Noah motions for me to get under the table, and when I do, he says, "I think I know what we can do."

A feeling of excitement spreads through me. "You do?"

"Yep."

"Let's hear it."

He squares his shoulders and draws himself up so he seems a little taller. "It's called the Secret Friendship Booth. We put a sheet or a blanket over a table, okay? Then two friends can go under and tell each other a secret. We charge everybody a quarter for one secret-telling and then we give the money to the school so they can buy some good stuff, like library books."

I tilt my head and stare at Noah. "Did your dad give you that idea?"

"No."

"Your mom?"

"No."

"You thought of that all by yourself?"

He nods solemnly.

"Wow . . . this definitely has possibilities . . . but don't you think we should have something on top of the table, like pictures of friends, maybe?"

"Maybe."

"Or little sayings about friendship?"

"We could print them from the computer," Noah suggests.

I wonder what the other kids are planning. "Well, maybe our booth won't be the most amazing one, but at least we'll have something." I give Noah a soft punch on his arm. "Hey, I thought you weren't good at coming up with ideas."

Noah shrugs. "It wasn't so hard, I guess." He glances toward the man with the laptop and the phone earpiece.

"Is that your dad?"

He nods.

"He works a lot too?"

Noah nods again.

"Your sister's on the skating team?"

"Yeah."

What if Noah's sister is the girl who is being mean to Becca? "Which one is she?" I ask.

"She's new. So they made her the alternate."

"Oh." Not the mean girl, then.

Noah squints at me. "Why do you ask so many questions?"

I remember when I asked Noah the same thing. "Are you making a joke?"

He bobs his head and lets out that croaky laugh.

I squint back at him and laugh too.

The next PHP time can't come fast enough; I'm so excited for Noah and me to get started on our booth. When the day finally arrives, I help Wanda carry twelve small jars of Play-Doh in neon and regular colors to the classroom but she won't tell me why. "You'll just have to see for yourself the night of the fair," she says mysteriously.

Claire is hauling a stack of library books and she won't say anything about her booth either. There are certainly a lot of secrets going around.

Tanya asks Mrs. Lamont, "Can Ash and I go out in the hallway to work in private?" She's holding a video camera.

Mrs. Lamont puts a hand on Tanya's shoulder. "Only if you won't disturb other classes."

"We totally won't." Tanya plucks Ashley by the arm as soon as we step into Mrs. Bezner's room. Today the two of them are wearing crocheted caps pulled down low over their long hair. "This is so fun!" Tanya exclaims. They let out their identical high-pitched giggles as they move toward the doorway.

I spot Noah. He isn't quite under his desk, but he's sitting on the floor in front of it. "Are you ready to get to work?" I ask cheerfully.

He doesn't answer, and he points to Mrs. Lamont, who is walking around the classroom in her bumblebee socks. He clamps his nose shut with his thumb and finger.

I smile. He starts to scoot backward under the desk.

"Noah." I take hold of his arm gently. "How are we going to print stuff off the computer if we're under your desk?"

His shoulders sink.

"I mean, it's nice under here and all, but . . ."

"There's no computer."

"Right."

He sighs.

"I bet it's not as hard as you think," I say.

He scrunches his mouth and looks at me. "How do you know?"

"You said you couldn't come up with ideas, and you did, right?"

"Yeah."

"So why not try something else you think you can't do?"

"This is different," Noah mumbles, wringing his hands. "Kids can tease you and stuff. And make you feel bad. And my idea, it's dumb. I thought about it some more. Everyone else's is better."

I narrow my eyes. "You're wrong about that. It is a good idea. And no one's going to tease you when you're with me." I stand up and reach for Noah's hand. "C'mon." After a minute, he takes my hand and lets me pull him up.

"Look"—I point—"there's a free computer in the corner. Let's get to work."

Noah and I spend the entire time searching for and printing sayings about friendship. We decide that we're going to glue them on a big display board and decorate it, and put it on top of the Secret Friendship Booth.

I don't even notice what the other kids are doing, because Noah and I are so busy. And I'm pretty sure that Noah isn't worrying about anyone else either.

"Calli," Noah says as I'm stacking up our papers. I realize it's the first time he's said my name. "I want to show you something."

Noah wraps his small hand around mine and tugs me back to his desk. This time, he sits down in his chair. I pull up a chair next to him. As he reaches into the pencil tray on the top shelf, I see a jumble of erasers and pencils and pens, all of them without caps, and along with those, several small light brown stones, all about the size of big grapes.

Noah takes one of the stones and holds it out to me. I feel like he's showing me a treasure.

"You can hold it," he says, and drops it into my open palm. The stone is smooth and has faint ripples of white across one end. I turn it over, then rub it between my fingers. I can't explain it, but somehow, holding it makes me feel calm all over.

"I like stones," he says. "That's what I do at recess. Look for stones."

Who is this kid? He likes to crawl under things, he can do a pretty good card trick, and he collects stones. Okay, so he can't make stuff and is awkward and weird. Does that mean something is wrong with him?

"Thanks for showing me." I give him the stone. He drops it back into his pencil tray, then turns to me. "We should put our own sayings in."

"What do you mean?"

Noah takes out a piece of notebook paper and pushes it toward me. "Write this down," he says, and hands me a pencil. "Friendship happens when you're not looking."

As I'm writing it down, I realize that I'm blinking to

hold back tears. I don't need to ask Noah if he's talking about me. I know he is.

I slide the paper toward him after I've finished, and he makes a hyphen, then slowly writes his name in shaky but strong letters. He adds the paper to our pile. "Now you." He hands me another piece of paper.

I stare at the blank white sheet.

"It's not as hard as you think," Noah Zullo says to me.

I look at him, with that spiky, messy hair and those crooked glasses and that little red mouth, and I write: *A real friend makes you feel special, no matter what.* Then I write my name.

"I like it," Noah says. "I like you."

I'm blinking again. "I like you too, Noah."

On the Bench

*a*fter school, Mom tells me, "We're dropping Becca at the rink, and then I'm driving you to the last improv class."

Becca doesn't talk to us the whole time in the van except to tell Mom to "watch the turns" because she's in the middle of putting on her eyeliner.

When she gets out, dragging her skating bag, she says, "I'm completely freezing," and Mom snaps, "Becca, deal with it." My sister flicks her hair and stomps toward the door of the rink.

"I don't know what's the matter with her these days," Mom remarks. "Teenagers!"

One pink and one blue Post-it note are on the steering wheel, and a yellow one is stuck to Mom's purse. I don't think she knows that there's a pink Post-it on the sleeve of her jacket.

As we get closer to winter break, the Calendar is looking a little less crowded, and Mom says it will be nice to have a couple of free days here and there.

In my room, I made my own mini calendar on the polar bear notepad I got from the dentist. I've been marking off the days until the Friendship Fair.

As we pull away from the skating rink, I clear my throat a few times before Mom finally asks, "Something on your mind, Calli?"

"Yeah," I say. "I was just wondering how everything's going to work out the night of the Friendship Fair. It's almost here. Have you thought about it?"

She digs one hand in her purse while steering with the other and pulls out a tissue. She dabs at her nose, then looks at me in the rearview mirror. "Well, Dad is going to take Becca to her competition, I will take Alex to the game, and I've asked Grandma Gold to meet you at the fair. I suppose you can walk over to the school by yourself. Grandma can't get there before seven. And, depending on how long the game and the competition run, we'll catch the end of the fair if at all humanly possible."

"Don't go to any trouble," I mutter, staring out the window.

"What?"

"Nothing."

Mom pulls up in front of the community center. "Grandma Gold will be there the entire time."

Great, I think, other people get their whole families; I get Grandma Gold. I don't even bother to say goodbye when I let myself out of the van.

As I'm walking down the hallway toward the improv room, all these thoughts about my family are tumbling around, and when I reach room seven, something happens. My feet don't stop at the doorway. They keep going. They keep going down the hall, past room nine and room eleven and room fifteen. There isn't a room thirteen, because it's bad luck. I end up way down the hallway by room nineteen and then I sink onto a bench. This time, blinking doesn't hold back my tears and they start dropping all over my jacket. There are a lot of them.

I don't want to go to the improv class.

I don't want to play silly games where I most certainly will get "out," or be partners with the hoodie kid or the girl with the little spiral, or learn about CLIC. I don't want to watch Liza wave around her fake glasses.

I don't want to be an actress.

So what I do is sit here. For the entire hour, on the bench. And I think about things. All kinds of things.

I think about how I'm going to explain to my parents that I cut the class. I think about Noah and how he came out from under his desk and how he talks to me and shows me things like his stones and a card trick and how

139

he doesn't wear his jacket inside anymore. I even think a little bit about Tanya Timley and her white teeth and imagine what it's like to be a model.

I think about how Noah and I are creating our booth for the fair but no one from my family even cares. Everything else seems more important to them. Even if we have the worst booth at the fair, that shouldn't matter, right? My family should be there.

But that's not how they are.

Then I wonder if I really am like Dad's lunatic sister, Marjorie. An outcast. The different one. Dad will be so mad at me for giving up and not going to the class. Like he's mad at Marjorie . . . Am I running away from something just like she did? Exactly why did she leave, anyway? Did her family make her crazy . . . like mine makes me crazy?

I think about that baby chick, and me hiding in the family photo, and even that old woman in the grocery store who I wanted to help, but Mom told me to "chop-chop."

I think about so many things all at the same time that I'm sure Noah would say I'm a bunch of mixed-up colors right now.

Noah . . .

I like you, he said. I like *you.*

Finally, at five o'clock, with no more answers than when I first sat down, I walk out the front door of the community center. Mom is late. I gather some dirty, crusty snow in my hand and try to make a snowball. The snow breaks apart, and when it does, there's a small brown stone sitting in my wet hand. I stare at the stone like it magically appeared to help me make sense of everything. But even when I rub it between my fingers, it doesn't seem to be working. I still feel all jumbled up.

When I see Mom, I slip the stone into the pocket of my jeans, then get into the van like nothing happened. She asks how the class was, and tells me Dad will want a full report. I say it was fine and I'm tired and I have a lot of homework and I'll tell her about it later.

Except that I can't. Every time I start to form the words that night, I feel guilty and ungrateful. Will she bring up the piano again? Then I'll end up feeling even worse. The entire night goes by without me saying a word. Fortunately, Dad is working late and doesn't have a chance to interrogate me. Just before I fall asleep, I promise myself that I'll think of a way to tell them I didn't go. I may have no talent, but I don't want to lie about it.

When I get to Noah's classroom the next day, he's absent. Mrs. Bezner tells me I can work on my own today. But I realize I don't want to work on my own.

Everyone is busy, chatting and coloring and cutting and gluing. The entire room is practically buzzing, but I have no one to talk to. Working on the project without Noah just doesn't feel right.

So it looks like I'm doing something, I take our display board from the pile on the side of the room and set it on top of Noah's desk, but I don't even bother to open it up. Even though his chair is too small for me, I sit down and start tapping my fingers on the display board.

Besides today, there's only one more working period before the fair, but Noah and I don't have that much more to do. I already brought in two old white sheets to hang over our table, and we're almost done with the display board. Noah brought in an empty plastic Cool Whip container and we cut out a slot on the lid for quarters. Then we made a sign: SECRET-TELLING—25 CENTS. ALL PROCEEDS WILL BE DONATED TO SOUTHBROOK ELEMENTARY SCHOOL.

Mrs. Bezner appears at Noah's desk and looks down at me with a kind face. "Everything going well, Calli?"

"I think so."

"Do you need any last-minute help?"

I shake my head. "We're okay."

"I know that Noah's been a bit of a challenge. . . ."

I shrug.

"But you seem to work fine with him." She smiles. "Well, just wanted to check in." Mrs. Bezner pats my shoulder and moves on.

I start examining the things in Noah's desk. I see the stones, and all the usual second-grade books—math, reading, social studies—and a few spirals.

I check to see if anyone's watching; then I flip open the spiral labeled NOAH ZULLO'S JOURNAL. His entries are very short, only one or two sentences on each page.

His printing is shaky and there are lots of misspelled words.

One page says *It was sunny today,* and another, *I don't like school.*

I keep reading until I get to one that says *I meeted Calli today.* My heart flutters, because the next line says *She is nice to me.*

That's it. I wish there was more, but he didn't write anything else.

I close the journal and carefully replace it under the other books.

That night at dinner, Becca is walking around the kitchen, all nice and helpful. When I sit down in my seat, Mom informs me that Becca set the table even though it was my turn. "Becca also chopped all the vegetables for the stir-fry," Mom says, "and she emptied the dishwasher. What's gotten into you, Bec?"

"Oh, just wanting to be a good daughter," she croons. Becca has a smile on her face, halfway sincere and halfway like she suddenly became my wicked stepsister.

"So, Calli," she says, sitting down across from me and scooping a big spoonful of stir-fry onto her plate. "How are things?"

"Fine," I say, uneasy. Since when is Becca interested in me?

She bats her eyelashes and even Mom is looking at her funny. "Tell me, how was your improv class yesterday?"

"Oh, yeah, Calli," Dad says, setting down the newspaper. "I got home too late last night to ask you. I'm anxious to hear. How was the last class? Any tinglings of the theater in your blood? What do you think?"

My heart starts to beat faster and my entire body grows hot and shaky. I wish that Alex was here but he has a late practice. He would make me laugh by knocking over his drink or burping continuously for two whole minutes.

Before I can decide how to respond, Becca announces, "How would she know? She wasn't there."

Mom frowns, looking confused. "What do you mean? Of course she was there. I dropped her off and picked her up at the community center."

"Ask her," Becca smirks. "Ask her if she was there." Then she smiles and crosses her arms. "Or ask Nathan."

"Nathan?" I manage to say. "What are you talking about?"

"His sister skates with me." When I don't say anything, she stares at me as if I am an idiot. "The boy who always wears that black sweatshirt."

I gulp as Dad looks back and forth from Becca to me. "Just exactly what is going on here?" he asks slowly.

All I can think is, the hoodie kid told on me? Some kid I don't even really know? Did he see me on the bench and realize that I skipped out of the class? Then he told his sister, who told my sister? Becca . . . I never said one word about what the coach said to her the night of the exhibition, and now she leaps at the chance to tell on me?

The three of them are staring at me, waiting for my answer. "Um . . ."

Mom sets down her fork. "Did you or did you not go to the improv class yesterday?"

"She didn't go," Becca says.

"I'm asking Calli," Mom says. Dad taps the table.

"Well," I answer, "here's the thing. I got there, and . . ."

"She didn't go," Becca says.

I hear Wanda's voice in my head. *Just tell them you hate it.*

"Calli?" Mom says.

They are all looking at me. *Just tell them.*

"She's right," I say, looking from Mom to Dad. "I did not go to the class." I eye my sister, who gives me a self-satisfied smile. "I was trying to think of a way to tell you."

Mom lets out a big surprised puff. "Where did you go?"

"I sat on a bench," I say.

"For the whole hour?"

"Yes."

"Calli, why would you do something like that?"

"Why would I do something like that? I'll tell you why." This is my moment. I can feel it. I only wish that Wanda or Claire could be here to witness it. I bolt up and a burst of words leaps from my mouth. From my heart.

"I don't want to play tennis or be the star goalie on a soccer team or get a black belt in karate! I'm not like the rest of you! I'm not golden! I don't have a special talent! I'm just plain old *average* Calli Gold. Isn't it okay to just be a good person and be who you are and not have to be great at something?"

Dad looks like someone punched him, and Mom is breathing loudly through her mouth, as if her nose stopped working.

"I'm sick of being number three with a 'C,' " I yell. "I hate the ABC game because I never have anything to say!"

"You just haven't found the right thing yet," Dad says.

"No, Dad, that's not it. You're not understanding what I'm saying."

"She's telling you she has no talent," Becca states. "Face the cold, hard facts."

I whip my head around and want to say many things to Becca, but all I can come up with is "Shut up, okay?"

"Don't say shut up to your sister," Mom scolds.

Dad shakes his head like he can't comprehend this. "Everyone has to be somebody."

"I am somebody!" I stamp my foot.

"Yeah," Becca pipes up. "Somebody who ditches a class her parents paid a lot of money for."

Slowly, Mom says, "Why didn't you tell us that you didn't want to take the improv class?"

"I did, but you didn't hear me. Nobody hears me! You just signed me up, remember?"

146

Dad clenches a muscle in his jaw. "Calli . . . is this what you really want? I have to admit, I'm disappointed. There's so much in this world to experience, so much out there, and you're choosing to settle for *ordinary?*"

"Ordinary is just fine, Dad, you should give it a try sometime!" I yell.

He slaps his hand on the table. "That's what I've spent my life trying *not* to be!"

I give him a stunned look. So does Becca.

"Larry Gold . . . who's he? Just Joel's little brother. Joel played basketball, got the girls, straight As, everything. My brother, the golden boy." He sits back in his chair. "Then there was my sister, the free spirit. Did whatever she wanted. Didn't care what people thought of her."

I stare at Dad.

"She really could have been someone! Where in the heck is New Zealand, anyway? What kind of a life could she have there?" he shouts.

I dig up the courage to ask something I've wondered for a long time. "Dad? How do you know anything about Aunt Marjorie? What if she's happy? What if she is someone she wanted to be?"

"Impossible!"

"Larry, take it easy," Mom says gently, and puts a hand on his arm.

He shakes his head. "Don't you see? I was just the invisible kid with nothing much going for me. I had to be somebody too! That's how you make your mark in this world."

There is a long silence until, finally, I say, "Dad . . . don't *you* see? I'm like you. Or you're like me. We're the same."

He looks at me—really looks at me—for a minute; then he looks away. "No. I told you. I wanted to be somebody. And I want my kids to be somebody too."

Becca smirks. "This family is so messed up."

I opened my heart to Dad and he didn't get it. This makes me all teary. I start to leave the kitchen; then I turn back. "I'm sorry I skipped out of the improv class, but I'm not going to be an actress, or anything else except a fifth-grade kid right now. And I bet if you asked Noah Zullo, he wouldn't say I'm ordinary."

"Who in the world is Noah Zullo?" Becca says as I'm running up the stairs.

"Just another ordinary kid," I scream, and then slam the door to my room.

I grab the jeans from yesterday that are hanging over my chair, and pull the stone from the pocket. I rub it between my fingers, but as smooth as it may be, the stone isn't making me feel calm at all.

The Wagon

*a*lex knocks on the door to my room later. "Got any tape?" he asks, leaning lazily against my doorframe.

I tuck a bookmark inside my book. "Why?"

"I need it for a project," he says. "Mom's all out. She used the rest of the roll when she was fixing the rip in the Calendar." He grins at me.

I get up and riffle through my desk drawers. I find a roll and toss it to him.

"Great," he says, and to my surprise, he spreads out a poster board on my carpet and starts laying out pictures, diagrams, and pieces of paper with typed words. "D'ya mind?"

"It's okay. . . . I was just reading."

"So," he says, arranging the items on the poster board, "I guess I missed the big scene."

"Yeah."

"You and Dad had it out?"

"Sort of," I say, then look down at the poster board. "What are you doing?"

"Some stupid project for biology. The results of my botany experiment."

"What was your experiment?"

"Giving plants water or Gatorade."

"Oh. What happened?"

"I don't know. The whole thing failed. Nothing grew."

"Don't tell Dad," I say.

"Yeah . . . I had an A going in that class, too."

Alex is still shifting things on the poster board when Becca flounces in. "Did you take my black tank top?"

"Me?" I answer.

"No, Alex," she says. "Yes, you."

"I'm not talking to you," I snap.

"Oh, what, you're mad?"

I glare at her. "Yes, I'm mad."

"They were going to find out anyway," she huffs.

"I wanted to tell them myself," I say.

"Well, I saved you the trouble."

I desperately want to say something she would say, like "You can leave now," but all I can come up with is "Why do you think I have your black tank top?"

"Because it's not in my closet, or the laundry, or my skating bag."

"I didn't take it."

"Well then, where is it?"

"How would we know?" I look down at Alex but he hasn't even glanced up.

Becca sneers at us, then stamps out.

Alex scratches his head. "Here's a scary thought," he says, his voice cracking. "You and I share the same genes with her."

"Pretty scary." I perch on the end of my bed. I realize that Alex has on shorts and a sleeveless T-shirt. "Aren't you cold in that?"

"Neh," he says.

His legs have gotten a lot of hair on them, and I can see some hairs on his upper lip too. For some reason, this makes me sad. He looks different with all that hair. "Hey, Alex," I say. "Do you remember when you used to pull me in the wagon?"

"Where should I tape this?" he says. "What, Cal?"

"The wagon? Alex? Do you remember?"

He shrugs and holds up a drawing of plant roots. "I don't know where to put this," he says. "I'm running out of room. I can't fit everything."

I glance down at his poster board. The frustrated look on Alex's face reminds me of Noah's when he says he can't make stuff. I kneel next to Alex and start moving a few items, and pretty soon, I've rearranged the entire layout.

"Hey, that's a lot better," he says, and reaches for the tape. He tears off a strip and tries to press the two ends together in a circle, then place it on the back of one of the drawings. The tape becomes crumpled and the drawing doesn't lay flat on the poster board. "I hate tape," he groans.

I laugh. "You do the tape; I'll put it on the poster board, okay?"

The two of us work in silence until all the items are neatly taped down. He stands up and takes a look at it. "What do you think? Not a bad poster for a failed experiment, huh?"

"I think it looks good."

"You want to know another thing I hate? Botany. Plants are the most boring things on earth," he admits.

"I love plants. And trees. Didn't you ever look up at a tree and feel completely amazed?"

He narrows his eyes. "To be honest, no."

"Well, I guess I can see how studying plants could get kind of boring."

"Kind of?"

I smile. "We haven't done plants yet this year. I think we do that in the spring."

He picks up the poster from the floor. "So you didn't like the theater class, huh?"

"Not really."

He raises his eyebrows. "I heard you cut."

"Yeah."

"And Becca told on you?"

I nod.

"She was wrong to do that," he says. "And hey, Cal, with Dad . . . I think he's got some, you know, issues."

I sigh. "He just doesn't get me."

"Well, number three with a 'C' "—Alex grins—"I think you're challenging him, and he doesn't know what to make of that."

"Me?" Quiet little me, challenging Dad? "I just didn't want to go to the improv class."

"Things will work out," Alex says. "Eventually. Okay, so, I gotta get to my algebra now. Thanks for helping me."

I find my place in my book. Alex walks to the door, then stops and turns. "Cal." He smiles at me. "I was just teasing you. I do remember the wagon."

A Person's Not a Puzzle Piece

For the next few days, Dad works late and doesn't make it home for dinner. Mom says he's starting a big project at work, but I wonder if he's avoiding me. The good thing: no ABC game. The bad thing: is he so mad that he doesn't want to face me?

Becca has extra practices before the competition, so she isn't around much either, and Alex is busy too.

One night, it's just Mom and me for dinner, and she makes us peanut butter and jelly sandwiches.

"This is kind of fun, isn't it?" she asks. "A change of pace."

"Yeah." I take a bite.

"I'm not used to all this quiet." She looks around the

kitchen. "So, here we are, just the two of us. You have me all to yourself. What should we talk about?"

I can't think of one thing. "I don't know."

"Polar bears?"

I shrug.

"Tell me about your fair."

"I don't feel like it right now."

She sighs. "Do you want to talk about what happened the other night?"

"Maybe."

She nods.

I stare at my sandwich. "Are you still mad I didn't go to the class?"

"I'm not really mad anymore, no," she says. "Disappointed, perhaps." She looks at me. "Not in you, I think, but more in the way the whole situation unraveled."

"Is Dad mad?"

She scratches her head. "He is, but to tell you the truth, more at himself than you. You touched a nerve. I knew he had some buried feelings about Joel and Marjorie and his childhood, but I didn't know how strong they were."

I shuffle the potato chips around on my plate. "Does he still want me to be an actress?"

She smiles. "I think he understands that's not in the cards right now." She shakes her head. "Families. We all know how to get under each other's skin, don't we?"

We finish our sandwiches. She takes our dishes to the

sink and rinses them. "Don't worry too much. Things will work out." At that moment, I realize how much she sounds like Alex.

When the Friendship Fair is two days away, we head to Mrs. Bezner's room for the final meeting. "This is it," Mrs. Lamont tells us. "Tie up all those loose ends, and put on your final touches. It's going to be completely wonderful!" She twirls and her long skirt billows out from her legs. I wonder which pair of insect socks she'll choose for the fair.

Claire is in a panic, because she doesn't think that she and her peer will have enough time to finish. "Why did we choose something so complicated?" she moans to me as we're walking. Wanda is in the back of the line next to Jason, of all people, and she's actually laughing at one of his obnoxious jokes.

"I'm sure it will be fine, Claire. You always worry, and then it always turns out okay."

She shakes her head. "We still have so much to put together."

I'm thrilled to see Noah at his desk. I practically push Tanya Timley out of the way and rush up to him.

"Where were you?" I demand.

He gives me that stare, the one he used to do when we first met.

"Is something wrong?" I sit down next to him on an extra chair.

156

"Yes, something's wrong."

"Well, what?"

He casts his eyes toward the floor. "I need to talk to you." He points under his desk. When we are underneath, Noah whispers, "I went back to the first doctor."

"Is that why you were absent?" I say.

He nods.

"So, do they know what's wrong?"

He wiggles his nose, then rubs at it. "They think it's something with my brain. It doesn't work exactly right."

"Your brain seems fine to me."

Noah sniffs. "This doctor, he kept showing me pictures and asking me what they were. They all looked like scribbles, so I said that. He wrote a lot of stuff down and I think it was bad."

"How do you know?" I interrupt.

Noah shrugs and continues. "Then he asked me to draw a picture of myself. You know I can't draw! So I made some lines and circles. He wrote more stuff down."

"What else did he say?"

"Like maybe I do have that syndrome. I can't remember the name. It might start with an 'A.' They think I need a helper in school."

"Oh." I nod.

"But you know what I told them? I said, 'I already have a helper and her name is Calli Gold.'"

"Noah," I say sadly, "I'm just a kid like you. I'm not the kind of helper they mean."

"I don't want a different helper," he says, and frowns.
I don't know what to say.

"The whole time, my mom, she just kept saying she wants me to fit in. What does that mean, anyway? A person's not . . . a puzzle piece."

I pat his knee.

"The world makes me nervous," Noah says.

"Why?"

"I can't explain it. It just does." He looks at me. "Don't you know what I mean?"

I think about the world for a minute. "Yeah," I say. "I do."

Noah starts wringing his hands. I watch him, then gently take his hands and cover them with mine. All I do is hold them for a few seconds until his hands become still. Then I let him go.

He pulls the corner of his lip into a sad half smile, and I wonder if a grown-up helper will know how to calm Noah's hands.

"Whaddya say?" I ask. "Should we finish our booth?"

"I don't know."

"Well, it's either that or stay under here for the rest of the day and try to figure out what's wrong with you."

He laughs. That croaky, rusty laugh, and I pull him out from under the desk. My heart is absolutely soaring, and I don't care about any other thing in the whole nervous world at that moment.

After Noah and I draw a few more decorations on our

board and glue on two final sayings, we take a step back and examine it together.

"I think it's great," I say. "I wouldn't add anything else."

Noah tilts his head. "It's good."

We sit down on the floor next to his desk. I stare at the classroom, at all the fifth graders and second graders working together. They all seem like they can hardly wait to show off their projects. I imagine all the families will be there, surrounding their children the night of the fair, complimenting them on their fantastic work. They'll probably take lots of pictures and bring them little presents and maybe even go out for ice cream afterward.

But all I can picture when I think about my family are Alex's and Becca's Post-its glowing on the Calendar, and how all of them will be at the game and the competition, not my fair.

Noah tugs my sleeve. "My dad bought me a new shirt for the fair."

"You'll look great," I tell him.

When it's time to go, Noah and I fold up our display board and put the sheets, the Cool Whip container, and our sign on top, then stick on a label that says NOAH ZULLO AND CALLI GOLD.

I pat Noah on the shoulder. "I'll see you at the fair."

"Okay." He gives me a thumbs-up.

Well, I think, Noah will be with me Thursday night. And Grandma Gold.

The Friendship Fair

Thursday afternoon, it begins to snow, and the weather people predict that we will get three to six inches before the night is over.

As soon as the first few flakes begin to swirl in the air, Jason calls out, "The snow's starting," and the whole class races over to the windows. We're all pressed against the cabinet, the heat radiating from the vents onto our faces, when Claire turns to Mrs. Lamont, who is watching the snowflakes along with us.

"They won't cancel the Friendship Fair, will they?" Claire asks.

"Oh, we're not going to let some silly ol' snow cancel our fair," Mrs. Lamont says. "All of you have worked way too hard for that to happen." She claps her hands. "All right, all right. I know you're very excited, but let's get back to our read-aloud book."

We settle back at our desks and Mrs. Lamont begins to read but I can hardly concentrate. I keep glancing at the snowflakes and thinking about the fair and my family and how Dad still isn't talking to me.

Actually, he is, sort of. He politely asks how my day was and if I have a lot of homework—but he's not really *talking* to me. He's not really talking much to anyone. Even though he started coming home at his regular time, he walks around quieter than I've ever seen him. He seems slower, like his usual energy has melted away. I'm worried about him and feel guilty, like I was the one who caused all the trouble.

After school, Mom keeps zooming into and out of the garage like a crazy person, driving Becca to practice, bringing Alex his basketball uniform because he forgot it, then racing back to the rink to give Becca her gloves. After I begged endlessly, she agreed to let me stay home while she was rushing around. When she comes back in, out of breath, she says, "I'm leaving again soon. You can walk over to the school by yourself when you need to go."

"I walk to school and back every day," I remind her.

"I know, but this is at night. It's dark out," she says.

"Mom, the school is a block and a half away. What's going to happen to me?"

She peels one blue and one pink Post-it from the Calendar. She takes off my yellow one about the fair and stares at it for a minute. "Remember to close the garage after you leave," she says.

"Okay."

"I've left a plate in the fridge for you to warm up. Some leftover pizza."

"Okay."

Her shoulders drop slightly. "I do feel so bad about this, Calli. Why does everything have to happen on the same night?" She picks up her purse and pulls out her keys. "You know, I don't think I realized this myself until this very moment, but sometimes . . . I feel as torn as that corner of the Calendar."

I squint at her. "What do you mean?"

"Here's a confession. . . . I just long for a day when I can sit at the front window with a cup of coffee . . . and not have to rush somewhere."

I nod.

She sighs.

"Sometimes you want to enjoy the gold without all the rush?" I say softly.

She gazes at me. "That's very insightful, Calli."

I smile at her. "Mom? Is Dad okay?"

She sighs again. "Well, my guess is he's doing a lot of thinking. He'll be fine." She looks at her watch. "We'll talk later. . . . I need to run," she says, kind of sadly. "Listen,

I will try to get there as soon as I can." She kisses me on the top of my head, then whizzes out of the kitchen, calling, "Zip your jacket all the way."

A little before six, I eat the pizza, rinse the dish in the sink, then put on my jacket. I remember to zip it all the way *and* close the garage. Big, floppy, wet snowflakes are coming down now, the kind you can really taste on your tongue, which is what I do the whole way to school. By the time I get there, my hair and eyelashes and jacket are entirely covered in snow.

In the gym, some people have already started setting up the booths. I see a table with the pile of Noah's and my stuff, but no Noah. I decide to wait so we can set up together.

Wanda runs up to me the moment she spots me, and pulls me toward her booth. Wanda and her peer called their exhibit Friendship Across the Universe. They used the Play-Doh to make all the planets, then set them up in order across a black poster board.

"Nice job with the planets," I say. "You matched the colors really well."

"Do you get our theme?" Wanda asks.

"Kind of."

I gather that Wanda and her peer have imagined that if there are beings living in another galaxy, we should try to make friends with them. Underneath their sign, FRIENDSHIP ACROSS THE UNIVERSE, they wrote *Aliens are our friends, not our enemies.*

"It's really creative," I tell Wanda. "And unusual . . . like you."

"Thank you." She grins at me, then crosses her arms. "Did you see Tanya's exhibit?" She points across the gym. There are Tanya and Ashley, with a TV on top of their table, and a gigantic sign that says SOUTHBROOK'S TOP MODEL COMPETITION.

"You've got to be kidding," I snort.

"Let's go over there." Wanda grabs my arm.

We saunter down the row of booths, waving to people and saying, "Great job," and "Good work." When we get to Tanya's booth, we stop. And stare.

First off, Tanya and Ashley are dressed up like they're going to a big party. Tanya is wearing a pink satiny dress and black high heels with skinny straps decorated with rhinestones. Ashley has on a white poufy lace dress and white party shoes.

"Wow," I say.

"Oh, hello." Tanya acknowledges us. "I know. Isn't our exhibit amazing?"

"I wasn't going to say that," I answer. "It's . . . very . . . bold."

"Mmm-hmm." Wanda rolls her eyes.

Tanya clasps her hands and I see that she has painted her nails a glossy pink. "We went with the model theme— you know, like *ANTM?*"

"Huh?" Wanda says.

"*America's Next Top Model.* My absolute favorite show

164

ever. Anyway, our whole idea is that competitors can really become BFFs." Tanya squeezes Ashley's arm.

"It's great." I try to make my voice sound as dull as possible.

Tanya turns on the TV and their video begins to play. First there is Tanya's smiling face saying, "Welcome, everyone, to Southbrook's Top Model Competition!" Next is a shot of Tanya, then Ashley, walking down a runway as if they're in a fashion show.

"We have to go now." Wanda pulls me.

The two of us break into a run, trying to hold back our giggles. Mrs. Lamont calls out, "No running in the gym!" and we slow down.

"What's up with them?" Wanda is laughing so hard that tears are brimming in her eyes. "Did they think that would demonstrate friendship? They look ridiculous! The whole thing is hilarious!"

"Leave it to Tanya to come up with something like that." I point toward Claire's table. "Hey, Claire's booth is looking good."

Wanda puts her hands up as if she is a crossing guard. "Claire's very hyper right now. She told me not to bother her until it's all set up."

"Okay," I say, and scan the gym. "Where do you think Noah could be?"

"I don't know. Listen, Cal, I have to go back and finish my booth. I'll see you later."

At six-forty, I decide that I have to start setting up

our booth even though Noah still hasn't showed up. I'm beginning to worry, but maybe they're just late because of the snow.

I spread the sheets over the table and leave an opening right in front. Then I unfold the display board and stand it on top of the table. I place the Cool Whip container and our sign in front of the board.

Our booth looks a little unexciting next to some of the others, but I know we have a good theme.

Noah still hasn't arrived. Maybe something really is wrong. He wouldn't miss the fair. He said he'd be here.

Just before seven, all the exhibits are set up. They are colorful and creative and unique. The gym looks as bright as a carnival. Somehow, even Tanya's model video fits in. Together, Mrs. Lamont and Mrs. Bezner pull open the gym doors.

The first one inside is Grandma Gold. She has on a gold sequined baseball cap and a thick red sweater. She walks right up to Mrs. Lamont and taps her on the shoulder. "I'm looking for my granddaughter. Calli Gold. I'm sure her exhibit is the best one in the entire fair."

Mrs. Lamont points in my direction and Grandma makes her way over. "Well, isn't this adorable?" She pecks me on the cheek.

"Hi, Grandma."

"So what are you supposed to do? Go under the table?"

"Yeah," I say. "And tell a secret."

"I don't think I could get these old bones under there."
She chuckles. "I'll leave that to you kids, but here, I'll
make a donation." She snaps open a zebra-print coin
purse and drops a quarter through the slot on the Cool
Whip container.

"Thanks, Grandma."

"Are you Calli?" It's the dad from the skating rink,
without his laptop and the phone attached to his ear. "I'm
Noah's dad." He pumps my hand.

"Nice to meet you."

"Dan Zullo," he says to Grandma Gold, and shakes
her hand too. "This is something." He whistles, looking
at the booth, shoving his hands in his pockets. "The
Secret Friendship Booth. Noah's been telling me about it.
Where is he, by the way?"

"I don't know. He was supposed to be here early to
help set up, but he didn't come," I say.

"What do you mean?" Noah's dad looks surprised. "I
dropped him off here an hour and a half ago."

"You did?" My mind starts to race and I feel all prickly
and nervous.

"Yes." Noah's dad looks around the gym. He wrings
his hands once, like Noah does sometimes, then drops
them to his sides.

"He's not in the gym," I say. "I'll check upstairs." I bolt
out the doors, up the stairs and dash into Mrs. Bezner's
classroom. I duck my head under Noah's desk.

He's not there.

I run back into the gym, which is now filling up with moms and dads, sisters and brothers, and grandparents. Everyone is buzzing and complimenting and snapping pictures, just like I imagined.

At Noah's and my booth, his dad is standing there looking very worried.

"Did you find him?" Grandma Gold shouts.

"No. You're sure he came in the school?" I ask Mr. Zullo.

"I watched him go inside. I told him I'd be back at seven." He pulls out his cell phone and begins pacing.

I stare at the sheets draped over our booth. I think I know where Noah is.

"Grandma." I clutch the sleeve of her sweater. "I need your help. Can you drive me somewhere?"

"Now?"

"Yes. Now."

"It's bad out there, Calli-kins. Snowing like the dickens!"

"It's important, Grandma. Real important."

Mr. Zullo covers the phone with his hand. "I'm talking to my wife. She's on her way but traffic's horrendous. I hope my daughter made it to skating. We sent her with another family so we could both be here for Noah."

He takes his hand away from the phone and continues talking. "He was doing better. I really thought he was improving. Maybe we should put him on that medication."

He puts the phone in his pocket; then he and Grandma

Gold start fretting about the slick roads and the snow and the notion that Noah might really be missing and where he could have gone. "He's probably somewhere in the school," Mr. Zullo says. "We can check all the rooms."

They're just standing there, discussing the situation in low voices, looking around the gym, as if this isn't urgent.

"Excuse me." I try to interrupt, but they don't hear. All of a sudden, I just can't listen to them anymore. I grab my jacket, run from the gym, then push open the front doors of the school. The snow pelts me in the face, but I start running faster, slipping on the sidewalk.

I can hardly see where I'm going but I know I have to try to get there. Where I think Noah is. At the end of the sidewalk, a car pulls up next to me and the window opens.

Grandma Gold's sequined baseball cap is all glittery and shiny in the dark. "Hop in," she yells. As I leap into the backseat, she presses her glossy red lips together, then opens her mouth wide and makes a popping sound. "'Help' is my middle name. The heck with the weather! What are grandmas for?" She clears the front window with the wipers. "Noah's dad is looking for him in the school. Where to, Calli-kins?"

"Turn right out of the parking lot," I yell as I snap on my seat belt.

"It's just like being in an action movie!" she exclaims. "Turn left!"

The car skids around the corner.

"Take it easy, Grandma! Now turn left again!"

Two more turns and straight ahead on Southbrook Road, and I can see it through the whirling snow.

The skating rink.

"Pull up in front, Grandma!"

She screeches to a stop and I jump out. The automatic doors part, and then I'm inside. The office is closed. I remember Mom said that Becca's competition was at a different rink. The banner with my sister's name glows eerily under a single spotlight. I can hear the sounds of a hockey game going on.

I reach the hockey-foosball table and bend down.

There, underneath, hidden inside a dark blue jacket, is Noah Zullo.

Helping Noah

I kneel down and gently touch the sleeve of his jacket. "Noah?"

Just like the first time, he doesn't answer.

"Noah, it's Calli."

"Go away," he whispers.

"No. I'm not going away."

"I want you to go away."

"Well, too bad. 'Cause I'm not."

He scrunches back so his eyes are peeking out from the collar of the jacket. "What do you want?"

"I want to know why you're not at the Friendship Fair. Noah, our exhibit looks great. Everyone's there. All the people from our classes. Mrs. Lamont and Mrs. Bezner. My grandma. Your dad."

"I'm not coming." His voice is small but certain.

I sit on the floor by Noah's shoes and glance toward the door. Grandma Gold is standing just outside the entrance, puffing on a cigarette. Suddenly, a question occurs to me. "How did you get here?"

"I walked."

"You walked here? From school?"

"Yeah."

"In the snowstorm? All by yourself?"

"Yeah."

"Noah, why?"

He peeks his entire face out from the jacket now and stares at me. His eyes are red, like he's been crying, and his skin looks paler than ever. "Because I didn't want to be at the fair."

We sit in silence for a few seconds. I see Grandma light another cigarette. "Are you going to tell me why?" I ask.

"Because it's bad."

"What's bad?"

"Our booth. My idea. Everything."

"It's not bad, Noah. I was there. Listen, our booth is at least as good as the other booths."

Noah rubs his nose. "No it's not. It's dumb. Everyone's probably laughing at it. And"—his voice cracks—"they're probably laughing at me too."

I crawl under the table, stretch out next to him, and prop myself up on my elbows.

"No one likes me," he says softly. "I hear them. They say I'm weird."

I don't know what to say. The two of us are quiet and I think I can hear Noah crying again.

"That's not true," I whisper. "I like you."

"You're different."

"So are you."

"That's the problem."

He sniffs. "Why can't they decide what to do with me? Doctors are supposed to have all the answers."

"I don't know. Even doctors don't know everything."

He sniffs again. "Then how will I ever be okay?"

It hits me then. Just like there are louds and quiets, there are kids like Noah. Maybe he has some kind of syndrome, and maybe he needs a helper, or maybe the world just makes him nervous, like he said. Or maybe not. Maybe he just is like he is. Different. Weird. But okay, in his way.

"Listen," I say. "I have something for you." I reach deep inside my jean pocket and pull out the stone I found when I ditched the improv class. I locate Noah's hand tucked inside his jacket sleeve and place the stone on his palm.

He doesn't even look at it. He rubs it between his fingers and blinks at me. Then, slowly, his lips pull into a half smile.

Grandma Gold comes barreling into the rink. "Calli?" she calls. "Where in the heck are you?"

I pull myself out and stand up. "Over here, Grandma."

When she walks over, I point under the table. "This is Noah. I found him."

"Well, what's he doing under there?" she asks. Her breath is smoky and bitter-smelling.

"It's kind of complicated."

She glances at me and looks back at Noah. "I'm no genius, but I have learned a few things in my seventy-odd years. Nothing ever gets solved by hiding under a table."

Noah squints at her.

"It's like the game of Scrabble, young man. You make your own words in this life. Don't look to anybody else to do it for you. You get what I'm saying?"

"Grandma," I start, but as I'm about to tell her to let me talk to Noah, that the situation has nothing to do with Scrabble, something incredible happens. Noah crawls out from under the table.

"Yeah," Noah says. "I get it." He turns to me. His hand is in a tight fist, but I know he's holding the stone inside. "Two people in this world think my idea is good, right?"

"Absolutely." I nod.

Grandma spits into her hand and tries to smooth down Noah's spiky hair.

"Grandma!"

"Oh, he doesn't mind," she scoffs.

He smiles up at her. "I like your hat."

"Young man," she says, "if I don't drive you and my granddaughter back to the school right now, we might be stuck here until morning."

The three of us look outside. It seems like an inch of

snow has fallen in the short time we've been inside the rink.

Noah takes a deep breath. "I'm ready to go now."

We all pile inside Grandma's car and she clears the window again with the wipers. "Oh, why didn't I spend the winter in Florida with my sister?" she wails.

"Because then you couldn't be in an action movie," I say, laughing. "Step on it, Grandma!"

"I always wanted to do that," she says cheerfully.

Noah looks at Grandma Gold in the front seat as she peers out of the snowy car window, her hat shooting little gold rays. "Mrs. Calli's Grandma?" he says.

"Yes?"

"You should stop smoking. It's really bad for you. Aren't you old enough to know that?"

She lets out a hoot. "It hasn't killed me yet. But I'll think about it. Thanks for reminding me, Mr. Calli's Friend."

When we get back to the school, both lots are filled and we have to park a block away. "It's a gosh-darn blizzard!" Grandma calls, and grabs Noah's and my hands. "Hang on for dear life!"

Noah's dad rushes up to him and gathers him in a big hug as soon as we get inside the gym. A woman—his mom, I guess—brushes the snow from his jacket and his hair. Then the two of them kneel next to Noah, looking very serious. Noah is gazing down while both of them grasp his arms, talking.

Mr. Zullo sees me over Noah's shoulder and mouths, "Thank you." Then he turns back to Noah, unzips his jacket, and takes it off, shaking out some of the wetness. Noah begins to finger a button on his shirt and I notice that his mom takes his hand away from the button, then glances around like maybe she's embarrassed.

He looks so good in his new shirt, all grown-up and proud. And they look like nice parents, just wanting to help their son. I wish that Noah had his deck of cards so he could show them that trick he knows, or that somehow, he could find the words to explain why he likes to collect stones, but all he does is stand blankly while they fuss over him.

Grandma Gold turns to me. "Want to walk around and see the other booths, cookie?" I nod as she takes my arm.

At Claire's exhibit, she and her peer are standing proudly in back of their booth, which is a detailed spread of what they've called Global Friendship. Only Claire, I think, would come up with something like this. She probably did the most research of anyone. They have photographs and items demonstrating how people express friendship in other countries.

"Claire," I say, shaking my head, "this is amazing. I think you're going to be president one day."

She beams and says, "I like your booth too."

Grandma Gold and I stop at some of the other booths, and as I make my way toward Noah's and mine, I cannot believe what I see. There's a line. A line of people waiting to visit the Secret Friendship Booth! I am in shock.

Not only that, but when I get to our table, I see that the Cool Whip container is filled almost to the top with quarters. Even some dollar bills are stuffed in. People are taking turns ducking under the sheet, and then coming out laughing or with serious looks or holding hands. Parents and kids, girls, boys, everyone is in line to tell a secret. Even Jason and the other uterus chanters are in line.

Mrs. Bezner is standing by our table. "Calli Gold!" she exclaims. "Where have you been? Your exhibit is the most popular one in the entire Friendship Fair!"

I am at a loss for words. I just shake my head and shrug. "I'm here now," I say finally.

Wanda is at my side, pulling my arm. "I've been looking for you," she says. "This is so much fun. Let's go under. I already told a secret with Claire. Now, you and me."

We wait for our turn. Finally, underneath the sheet, all the noise from the gym is muffled. The voices sound far away, and the air is warmer and more still. It's almost like we're underwater in our own private little world. Wanda and I can't see anyone except each other, and it feels cozy and, somehow, magical.

"Can I go first?" Wanda asks.

"Sure."

"Now, what's said in the Secret Friendship Booth stays in the Secret Friendship Booth, right?"

"Absolutely."

She leans toward me, close to my ear, and whispers, "I'm wearing a bra."

My eyes widen. "You are? I thought your mom said you couldn't get one."

"When I told her we were going to start the puberty unit in health, she said it was time."

"Wow. How does it feel?"

"Weird. Good. Grown-up. I don't think it fits me right yet, though." She glances down at her shirt, then says, "Now you."

"You're my best friend."

"That's not a secret. That's a fact."

"Okay . . . I think I helped someone who was really sad."

"Who?"

"Noah Zullo."

"That's pretty cool, Calli. It really is. I mean it. What was he sad about?"

"That's his secret." I look down at the floor. "But I guess what I did . . . it's not like being a star in an improv show, huh? Or shooting the winning basket, or getting first place in skating."

"Forget about all that." Wanda takes my hand. "You know what you did."

"You're right," I say as we come out from under the booth. "It's just hard."

Tanya Timley is standing in front of us. Her face is

red and there are blotches of mascara underneath her eyes. "No one is coming to my booth," she sniffles.

"Oh, get over it, Tanya," Wanda snaps.

Tanya huffs at Wanda and turns to me. "I don't get it. Go under a sheet and tell a secret? What's the big deal?"

"It's fun!" Wanda says.

"Yeah," I add. "You want to go under? There's no line right now."

"I don't think so." Tanya looks away. "I left Ashley alone."

"Maybe later," I offer.

Tanya's lip trembles but then she swings her hair and stomps away, heels clicking noisily on the gym floor.

"'No one is coming to my booth,'" Wanda says, imitating Tanya's high voice.

"You're the best, Wanda." I watch a mom and dad duck under the sheet with their daughter, a second grader from Mrs. Bezner's class. I let out a big sigh.

Wanda nods. "You have a right to be mad. It stinks, you know."

"What does?"

"That your family isn't here."

"I guess."

"There's still time. Maybe they'll show up. How long could a basketball game and a skating competition take?"

I shrug so it looks like I don't care. "Let's have some cookies," I say, and the two of us go find Claire.

Calli's Passion

*A*s Wanda, Claire, and I are sitting on the floor in the refreshment area, eating chocolate chip cookies and drinking fruit punch, the same feeling comes over me that I had when the three of us went sledding. I look around the gym, at all the booths and the people, wrapped in the snug, winter-warm glow surrounding us all. I found Noah, and my two best friends in the entire world are right by my side. Maybe that's enough. I want to hang on to this moment forever.

"WC Squared," I say, and reach my hand into the middle of Wanda, Claire, and me. They pile their hands on top of mine, and we say together, "WC Squared."

"No matter what happens in junior high," Claire says.

Wanda starts giggling, and I hear several loud burps behind me. Then I feel a light kick on my back and turn to see two enormous basketball shoes. When I look up, my heart soars, the same as when Noah laughs. My brother is towering above me, holding a bottle of grape Fanta, his favorite soda pop, and burping, as Grandma Gold would say, as if there is no tomorrow.

I leap up. "You're here!"

"Cal, I wouldn't miss this." Alex is sweaty and covered with melting snow but I hug him anyway. He's still wearing his basketball uniform. "I wanted to leave the game early, but Dad wouldn't let me. Mom dropped me off. She was mad; there weren't any parking spaces." He takes a huge gulp from the bottle and burps again. Wanda bursts into a new fit of giggles.

A surge of happiness skips across my heart again. "Alex, I'm really glad you came."

"So show me your booth already." He grins.

I pull Alex over to the Secret Friendship Booth. On the way, I tell him about Noah and how he came up with the idea, the display board with our own sayings added in, and the pile of money we've collected. "We're donating the money to the school library. Mrs. Lamont was going to count it a little while ago. I wonder how much there is."

"Cal." Alex looks over the booth, nods, then gives me a light punch on my arm. "Pretty good job here. Everyone seems to like it. You should feel really proud."

"I do," I say. And I whisper it again to myself. "I do."

Just then, Mrs. Lamont and Mrs. Bezner, who are

standing in the middle of the gym with a microphone, call for everyone's attention.

"If we can have just a minute of your time . . ." Mrs. Lamont is saying. I realize that she is wearing real high-heel shoes tonight, and she has on sheer black tights instead of insect socks.

"We're so glad that all of you are here tonight." Mrs. Lamont's voice echoes across the gym. "Thank you for braving the snowstorm to share this wonderful occasion with my fifth-grade class and Sherri Bezner's second-grade class."

A few people clap; then Mrs. Lamont continues. "When Mrs. Bezner and I first came up with the idea of a fair devoted to celebrating friendship, we weren't sure how it would turn out. But I think you can agree that our students have worked very hard, and our Friendship Fair is an undeniable success!"

Now a lot of people clap, and some whistle.

"Every single exhibit tonight is special." Mrs. Lamont gestures in a wide circle. "But there is one particular booth I do want to mention because of its simple, heart-felt message."

Wanda sprints over to me and I feel all jittery inside. Is it possible that Mrs. Lamont is talking about Noah's and my exhibit?

Mrs. Lamont opens her mouth to continue, but then the sound of a slamming door reverberates from outside the gym. Everyone hears when someone yells, "Well, it's about time you got your shameful behinds down here. What's wrong with the two of you, missing this important night? Don't look at me like that, Larry! I'm still your mother and I can still lecture you if you need to be lectured."

Of course I know that voice, and of course I know who Larry is. I'm filled with a jumble of embarrassment and shock and happiness as the gym doors burst open. I step behind Wanda, and when I peek over her shoulder, I see Mom, Dad, Becca, and Grandma Gold marching into the gym as if everyone was waiting for their arrival.

Everyone stares at them for a second and they stare back. The entire gym seems as frozen as the snow outside. Mom's mouth hangs open in a small O. Dad has his hands on his hips. Becca is wearing her new skating costume and curly ponytail but her eyeliner is smudged and she looks like she's been crying.

"Sorry to interrupt," Mom says politely.

Mrs. Lamont clears her throat and nods at Mom. "As I was saying, one of our booths tonight has made us all— young and old—remember the very special feeling of sharing a secret with a friend."

I can hardly breathe as Mrs. Lamont says, "Calli Gold and Noah Zullo? Can you both raise your hands?"

I'm at one end of the gym and Noah's at the other, but we both slowly put our hands in the air while Mrs. Lamont goes on. "Calli and Noah's booth not only portrays the beautiful meaning of friendship, but they raised twenty-seven dollars and fifty cents for our school library."

People start clapping. I see Dad punch his fist into the air and hear him shout, "That's my daughter! She's a Gold!"

Mrs. Lamont waits until the clapping stops. "Please enjoy the rest of the fair tonight, and, again, thank you for coming. Oh, and drive safely!"

I'm still standing right in front of the Secret Friendship Booth with Alex and Wanda as Mom, Dad, Becca, and Grandma push their way toward me. Mom almost flattens someone with her purse as she barrels through the crowd. I touch Wanda's arm. "Don't leave." She nods.

In another second, they're all next to me, Mom and Dad crushing me with hugs and shouting in my ear. "The best exhibit in the whole place." Dad beams. "There wasn't a doubt in my mind!" He's acting like himself again.

Mom dabs at her nose with a tissue. "We are so proud of you." She glances at Becca. "Aren't you proud of your sister?"

"Sure," Becca sighs.

Mrs. Lamont makes her way over to the booth.

"All this time," Dad says, "we've been signing you up for all those extracurricular activities, sports and what-not." He smacks his forehead with the palm of his hand. "I should have known. Why didn't I see it? You have a head for business." He grins and pokes me with his elbow. "Just like your old man." He winks at Mrs. Lamont.

He bends down, inspects the booth, and taps his knuckles on the tabletop. "I'm very impressed," he says. "Terrific concept."

"Thanks, Dad," I say.

"Maybe you'll start your own business one day," he continues. "We can kick around some ideas. Lots of kids like you get going pretty young."

"Dad . . . I'm not starting a business right now." I knew he wouldn't hear me, so I say it louder, as loud as any other Gold. "Dad, listen to me. I'm not starting a business. This is just a school project. I think it's pretty good for what it is."

"It's not pretty good," Mrs. Lamont pipes up. "It's great."

"Besides," I say, "it wasn't even my idea. It was Noah's. He was the one who came up with the whole thing."

Dad looks startled, taking in the fact that a Gold isn't behind the idea. "It doesn't matter who came up with the idea," he says at last, "it's what you do with it."

I can feel Wanda's breath on my cheek, she is so close to me. "What I want to do," I say, "is have the memory of how everyone had so much fun tonight and how they shared secrets with each other. I think that's enough."

Mrs. Lamont is smiling at me. She turns to my parents. "I hope you know that you have a very special daughter here."

Dad cries, "Of course we do!" Then he chuckles. "You know, we pride ourselves on achievement in the Gold family. We've been a little worried about Calli, I'll admit, because she doesn't seem to have found a passion like her brother and sister."

Out of the corner of my eye, I see Alex shake his head.

"Oh, I think she has a passion," Mrs. Lamont says, putting her arm around my shoulders. "You could call it *compassion*." She looks down at me. "Do you know what that means, Calli?"

"Sort of."

"Concern for others," she says. "Putting their needs and feelings before your own. Understanding that sometimes, another person is more important than yourself." She looks across the gym toward Noah, then turns back to Dad. "It's not the kind of thing you can learn in a class. It's just in here." She taps her heart.

For a moment, we all stand there, quiet. Finally, Mrs. Lamont waves to Mrs. Bezner across the gym. "Excuse me now. It's certainly been nice to visit with you."

My eyes meet Dad's but we don't know quite what to say.

Grandma Gold breaks the silence. "Enough with the schmaltziness here, let's get a picture." She pulls her camera from her purse and motions me toward the booth. "Go stand in front."

I take a few steps toward the booth, then stop. "I need Noah. Noah has to be in the picture too."

He's still across the gym, and his parents are walking

on either side of him as if they think he'll suddenly decide to run away again. I stride over.

"Can I get a picture with Noah?" I ask his parents. "In front of our booth?"

His mom is holding tightly to his hand. "I don't know," she says hesitantly.

"It's fine," Noah's dad says. "Let him go over there."

After a moment, she places Noah's hand in mine carefully and gently, like she's handing over something breakable.

"You okay?" I ask him as we're walking toward the booth. His parents are a few steps behind us.

He shrugs.

"You look really good in the shirt."

"I do?"

I nod and gesture to the booth. "Look," I say. "Noah, look what you did."

The two of us stand and watch people ducking into and out of the sheet.

"Uh-uh." He shakes his head. "Look what we did."

"Am I ever going to get this picture?" Grandma Gold calls.

I tug on Noah's hand and we stand in front of the booth, him on one side of it, and me on the other. As Grandma snaps the picture, I think about the family photo on my dresser and Noah under the hockey-foosball table. I realize that neither one of us is hiding anymore.

At last, the night is winding down, and people are starting to leave. There's no one in line at the booth. I turn to Mom and Dad. "Do you want to go in the Secret Friendship Booth with me?"

Wanda gives me a thumbs-up as I part the opening between the sheets and my parents and I duck under the table. We sit down cross-legged.

"It's a little cramped in here," Dad observes.

"Larry," Mom scolds, then turns to me. "So what do we do?"

"We tell each other a secret," I say. I draw in a deep breath. "I'll go first." My words tumble out in a rush. "I'm not sure I fit in with our family."

"Oh, honey, that's not true," Mom says, leaning toward me, her eyes sad.

"I'm not like the rest of you. I don't do anything special. And you're disappointed in me. You said it that night . . . when I didn't go to the improv class."

Dad straightens his back and bumps his head on the table. "Ow." He strokes a spot on the back of his head. "Calli, all I really wanted was for you to find something you love to do."

Mom is nodding. "And after tonight, after what your teacher said about you, how could anyone say you're not special?"

"I'm not, though," I answer. "I'm just regular. And I think that's okay." I take another breath. "Do you?"

Mom creases her eyebrows together. "Yes," she says. "Of course." She looks at Dad.

He nods, then taps the underside of the table. "But I still think you—"

"Dad . . ."

"Okay, okay."

"Here's another thing," I say. "Can we stop doing the dinnertime ABC game?"

He looks pained now. "You really don't like it?"

"I really don't like it."

He sighs but doesn't answer.

"I have a secret," Mom whispers, and winks at me.

"Tell," I say.

"I've signed up for piano lessons."

"Oh, Mom!" I inch toward her and give her a hug. "That's great!"

"What?" Dad exclaims. "Karen, how are you going to have time to learn to play the piano?"

"I'll make time."

I glance at Dad. "Do you have a secret?"

"Me?"

"Why not?"

"A secret . . . Well . . ." He turns to me and I'm surprised to see a sorrowful look in his eyes. "I have several. Maybe too many to reveal under this table. I've been doing a lot of thinking, and . . . you were right . . . about a lot of things. Marjorie, for starters . . . How do we know she's not exactly who she wanted to be? You know something? None of us ever asked her."

Mom nods.

"And Joel," he says. "I wasted a lot of time trying to live up to my brother when I could have just been myself."

Mom and I wait. Then she says, "Anything else?"

He ruffles my hair and shakes his head. "I disagreed with you that night when you said it, but you *are* like me. We're more alike than I ever realized. I kept trying to push things on you, but you were always just fine the way you were." He sighs. "In a way, Calli Gold, I think you've got it all over the rest of us."

Home

The snow has just about stopped and Grandma Gold insists on driving home. Dad helps her clear off her car. She settles herself inside and waves goodbye. "It'll probably take me hours to get home. If you don't hear from me by tomorrow, call the police!"

The five of us start walking through the snow. "We left the cars in the garage," Dad tells me. "The lot was full, plus it was easier to walk through this stuff than drive."

Alex's cell phone rings and when he answers it, covering the phone with his hand, Mom says, "Who's calling you now?"

Alex pulls the phone away from his mouth and grins. "My, uh, girlfriend."

Dad stops and looks at Alex, who shrugs. "There's more to life than basketball, Dad," he says happily, and strides ahead of us.

Becca has barely said a word the entire night, and now Dad puts his arm around her. "I'm sorry," he says.

"I'll live," she drawls.

"What happened?" I ask.

Becca turns to me. "I didn't skate, okay? Not a huge deal."

"You didn't skate?"

"The coach put in the alternate," Dad says.

"Which was fine with me," Becca interrupts. "But then Dad had to go and yell at Coach Ruth, in front of everyone. Dad, you know, your screaming was worse than the fact that I didn't skate."

"What can I say?" Dad mumbles. "I got a little crazy when I didn't see you out there on the ice. You're good, Bec, you're a part of the team."

"Dad," Becca says, stopping him. "It was the right decision to put in the alternate. Even though she's new to the team, she's . . . a better skater. The coach has basically been telling me that all season, but I didn't have the guts to tell you."

Dad looks crushed.

I remember that the alternate is Noah's sister and I glance at Becca. For just one second, she catches my eye with a not-so-mean look.

Alex trots back to us and says, "What did I miss now?"

Mom shakes her head. "Oh," she sighs. "Just some honesty."

"You'll work harder," Dad says. "I'm sure you can earn your spot back."

"You know," Becca says, "to tell you the absolute truth, I'm not sure I want to."

We all look at Dad standing there like his entire family has turned against him, snowflakes dotting his hair and his jacket.

"Larry?" Mom says softly.

He nods at Becca. "If that's what you want," he says. "It's okay with me."

As we start walking again, I don't even mind that I'm not by myself and can't do my usual thinking. There's something different with my family. I can feel it.

I look at them all—Becca flipping her hair, Dad with his arm around her, Mom swinging her purse, and Alex in his basketball shorts—and I realize that what Mom said is true: they are my family, and they're under my skin, like it or not.

One thought comes to me, though, as I'm watching all of them tromp through the snow. I am a sort of a muse. In my own way. And that's a pretty good thing to be.

Afterward

Things happen in funny ways. Or I should say things change in funny ways.

One week after the Friendship Fair, Alex's team lost in the semifinals. Dad really did cry this time. He was a lot more upset about it than Alex, who was more concerned about coming up with a creative way to ask his girlfriend to winter formal.

I asked him, "Is she one of those silly cheerleaders?"

He said, "No. In fact, she reminds me a little bit of you."

Becca told my parents that after this year, she's definitely done with the skating team.

"Then I guess I'm done with the costume committee," Mom said.

"This whole family's falling apart," Dad moaned.

"Not falling apart," Mom said, "just reorganizing itself. For the better. More gold, less rush."

I know Mom is secretly happy about the prospect of having fewer Post-its on the Calendar in the future, except for the new green ones. They all say *Mom—Piano Lesson.* The other day, she even had time to wash the minivan. I hope that someday soon, I'll spot her at the front window with a cup of coffee when I'm coming in from school.

At first, it looked like Dad didn't know what to talk about at the dinner table after we stopped doing the ABC game. So one night, I brought up my worries about the polar bears. We discussed it for the whole time! No one mentioned any achievements, unless you count Mom telling us about learning to play her first Broadway show tune.

Grandma Gold put the picture of Noah and me in a frame and gave it to me. We both have proud, happy smiles. Before everything happened at the Friendship Fair, I was considering stuffing the one of my family into a drawer, but I decided not to. I put the one of Noah and me right next to it on my dresser.

Mrs. Bezner asked me to work with Noah on a regular basis, even though the Peer Helper Program is over for now and he has an aide helping him. Twice a week at recess, I go upstairs and read stories with him and just hang out and talk. I think I might even want to be a teacher one day.

But I promise I won't wear socks with insects on them and take my shoes off in the afternoon.

Or maybe I will.

One thing's for sure. I know I can raise my voice when I need to. I am a Gold, after all.

Acknowledgments

Writing a book has been a dream of mine since I was young and I am still in disbelief that my dream has come true. To say that this was a journey is a grand understatement. There were many bumps along the road, times I wanted to throw in the towel, and moments of pure insanity. I am grateful beyond words to my editor, Caroline Meckler, and to Wendy Lamb, for seeing the light and joy in this story and for their advice, questions, and editing; to Vikki Sheatsley for her wonderful cover design; to my agent, Jennifer Flannery, who called me on a cold March afternoon when she was only on page fifty-eight, and whose support of this book never, ever wavered, not even in my most doubtful days; to my soul sister, Lauren, who has been a steadfast listener and provided ongoing encouragement and enthusiasm (what would I do without our lunches?); to the members of my mother-daughter book club, the Bookie Buddies, who openly shared what they liked and didn't like about the books we read; to my mom, who always said she was

197

my biggest fan (I so dearly wish you were here, but somehow, I know that you are); and to my dad, who I am so very much like and who showed me what it takes to achieve a dream. My heart is filled with love for my four anchors, who keep me afloat amidst the craziness: Ben, who listens endlessly, even when he's falling asleep, does my taxes, and puts up with my cobralike intensity; Rachel, whose maturity and insight go way beyond her years; Sam, the inspiration for Calli's brother, with his even temperament and constant ball-playing in the family room; and especially Cassie, my first reader and real-life muse, who reminded me what was funny, and was absolutely positive from day one that this was "a book."

It can be a challenge to find your voice within a family. Stay true. Like Grandma Gold told Noah, "You make your own words in this life. Don't look to anybody else to do it for you." Always believe that you can, and you will.

About the Author

Michele Weber Hurwitz grew up in a suburb of Chicago and still lives in the same area with her husband and three children. She does not have a huge calendar taped to her kitchen wall but has been known, on occasion, to drive with Post-it notes stuck to the steering wheel. This is her first novel.

Visit her at micheleweberhurwitz.com.